G. Bruno Denoncourt is a Canadian actuary. With a Bachelor of Science diploma from Laval University and his Fellowship of the Casualty Actuarial Society of USA, G. Bruno worked all his career inside insurance companies and as a consultant. *The Manhattan Smugglers* is his first published novel. He is working on Part-2, and maybe for a trilogy. G. Bruno loves geography and history. He travelled much, visited more than 20 US states, and many parts of the world. G. Bruno worked in Manhattan during several months. Presently, he lives in Montreal, Canada.

To my parents.

G. Bruno Denoncourt

THE MANHATTAN SMUGGLERS

AN INTERNATIONAL INTRIGUE THROUGH RUSSIA, UKRAINE AND MORE

Austin Macauley Publishers™
LONDON • CAMBRIDGE • NEW YORK • SHARJAH

Copyright © G. Bruno Denoncourt 2023

All rights reserved. No part of this publication may be reproduced, distributed, or transmitted in any form or by any means, including photocopying, recording, or other electronic or mechanical methods, without the prior written permission of the publisher, except in the case of brief quotations embodied in critical reviews and certain other non-commercial uses permitted by copyright law. For permission requests, write to the publisher.

Any person who commits any unauthorized act in relation to this publication may be liable to criminal prosecution and civil claims for damages.

This is a work of fiction. Names, characters, businesses, places, events, locales, and incidents are either the products of the author's imagination or used in a fictitious manner. Any resemblance to actual persons, living or dead, or actual events is purely coincidental.

Ordering Information
Quantity sales: Special discounts are available on quantity purchases by corporations, associations, and others. For details, contact the publisher at the address below.

Publisher's Cataloging-in-Publication data
Denoncourt, G. Bruno
The Manhattan Smugglers

ISBN 9798886936087 (Paperback)
ISBN 9798886936094 (ePub e-book)

Library of Congress Control Number: 2023911925

www.austinmacauley.com/us
First Published 2023
Austin Macauley Publishers LLC
40 Wall Street, 33rd Floor, Suite 3302
New York, NY 10005
USA

mail-usa@austinmacauley.com
+1 (646) 5125767

I would like to thank Austin Macauley for their support and the publishing of the book.

Table of Contents

Preface	11
The Collapse	13
Jonathan's Youth	25
Murky Guys at the Bar	39
Few Days Off and Discussion with Mom	68
The Red Sea, Sudan, and Amanda	78
Central Park	86
Brown Envelopes	103
The Catskills	142
Killings in Smolensk	167
Fierce Crooks	195
Istanbul, Turkey	204
In Africa	213
A Round of the "Beef Game"?	214

Preface

In 2011, I had the chance to work in Manhattan for several months. I had started this thriller, based on my visit, including in two or three chic Manhattan resto-bars.

So, I got inspired by that, using my quite extensive geographical, political, historical and economic knowledge, especially about Russia, the Soviet Union and its former republics, including Ukraine. Part of the action takes place in Russia and Ukraine, against the background of the Russian-Chechen civil war, around 2010 and before. And Jonathan, it's a bit me.

I wrote the core of the text that follows from 2011 to 2015; it then slept, so to speak, from 2016 to 2020. Then I met my wife, in 2020.

She strongly encouraged me, in early 2021, to take up this work, bring it to its final version, and publish, in English and in French. It was done, at the beginning of February 2022. Without too much pretension, for the fun of it. My wife is preparing her own thriller. I support her and work with her on it.

Then Russia invaded Ukraine, on February 24, 2022.

Friends and early readers seemed pretty unanimous, their comments going something like this:

1) *Your story is very good, we loved reading you!*
2) *You hit the nail on the head, with a thriller partly set in Russia and Ukraine, and your lot of historical, economic and political references.*
3) *There are still too many typos, you should correct that, the layout needs to be improved; take care of it, and publish again soon!*
4) *You should add some maps, too!*
5) *The end leaves us wanting more... when is the next book, Part 2, is Gerry coming back, is Billy dead, are you going to draw inspiration from the war in Ukraine...? When?*

I reworked, I had the items in point 3 revised, but copyright free geo maps, with good resolution: too complex for now. I encourage readers to go on the web, once in a while. So here is version 2.

And for Part 2? I started it in March 2022. With more vocabulary, more adjectives, many surprises. And a trip to Turkey, Romania or one of Ukraine's neighbors, maybe... if the situation is not too risky, soon in 2023 to gather some inspiration? With a friend, we are seriously thinking about it. But it's a part-time job for me. So, see you soon, dear readers!

G. Bruno Denoncourt
April 10, 2023

The Collapse

Jonathan Winkler was sitting at the bar, having a Johnny Walker, conversing.

It was June 4, 2010, Friday night.

He'd finished his second Master's in International Economics, from Vermont State University, USA, and was not such a young man, in his 40s.

He was just coming back from this long haul through lectures on world economy, financial mathematics and blistering, long nights, writing papers on price elasticity of demand and supply and other esoteric stuff.

Before, Winkler had worked many years in various US cities, such as Chicago, Boston, New Orleans, and San Francisco, and for several large insurance companies and banks. Reeling from difficulties because a new CEO couldn't keep it together, the last bank he worked for closed down his department. That's when he decided to go back to school.

The bar was the prestigious, mysterious, glorious DD bar in midtown Manhattan, the very heart of the heart of New York City and very close to the world-famous Waldorf Astoria hotel.

Where many UN dignitaries went for a drink to end their day, some to start it, many to finish talks that would influence the whole world.

This evening, however, the oak walls bar was not full of dignitaries, not at all, but very crowded with New York's finest in law and business, healthcare and engineering and, of course, Wall Street's best brokers, honest or not.

Winkler was talking with a military from Montana and a pretty woman, a nurse, from Delaware. Behind them, at a table, he could hear a conversation between four middle-aged engineers from South Africa, on holiday in Manhattan. Winkler could catch snippets: something about a big international oil and gas project. Their voices carried over the general din.

Billy, the main bartender, was, as almost always, completely busy. Rolling out all types of drinks with the ease of a circus juggler. He was pouring out an easy on-tap beer in front of Winkler, when, suddenly, he collapsed.

Winkler immediately jumped over the bar, breaking some glasses and bottles, to help. It looked like a heart attack. The next minutes would prove a turning point for Billy, and in Winkler's life.

Billy was lying on the floor, convulsing, his body contorting as if he were dancing disco. His eyelids were shuddering, as he pulled Winkler down toward him and spoke weakly.

— Prince Marty, the Third.
— Prince Marty, the Third?

Winkler had no idea what was being said to him, so earnestly, in whatever voice Billy the bartender had left.

Billy was breathing with difficulty. His eyes, though, were very intense, focused on Winkler, and he was still firmly holding on to his arm.

— Yes, Prince Marty the Third. He should come tomorrow, or soon. He has very, very dirty plans. Nefarious.
— Plans? What do you mean? A Prince? But you're only a bartender. Don't worry, we have to take care of you first.
— Don't say this, young man, I'm not "only a bartender." I have been working here for more than twenty-five years; I know many people, all kinds, I know about… know about so many nasty things and secrets, Marty… the rev…

But his voice weakened, as his lids fell, his head dropped to the side.

At the same time, very quickly, three or four men working in the bar were there to manage the situation. The scene turned into a battlefield. A tall man, who apparently was the manager of the DD that night, came over, in a running sweat and literally bumped Winkler away from the bartender.

Was there something he didn't want Winkler to hear?

Clearly, the manager had an interest in keeping clients on site, keeping things going, "business as usual" and all that, but looked concerned for Billy, too.

— The ambulance is coming! he shouted to people sitting at the bar. Everybody, stay calm, please. He will be fine. Don't disturb your evening; he will be fine! Please go back to your evening.

The strategy worked. In fact, not so many people had noticed Billy's fall, and they couldn't see him behind the bar.

So, dignitaries, physicians, businessmen, nice ladies, local politicians, unknown mafia guys, professors, students, blue collars, half drunk or not so drunk, started to chat again, got back to their phones, the closest ones taking a look at Billy, but not much more.

The three other guys took Billy away on a stretcher to the ambulance.

Some clients were looking attentively, others not at all, attending instead to their own table or few inches of the bar, while Billy's cortège went through.

The bartender was still unconscious and not moving. The manager immediately took Winkler apart.

— What did he tell you exactly? Who are you?
— Jonathan noted the word "exactly."
— What? I'm only a client. I don't know. He told me to call the boss, the ambulance, the doctor, the hospital, to help, in a word. I did.
— Okay, fine, many thanks, now you have to go, get back to your friends. I have to work, as you probably understand.
— Perhaps... well, you need a good bartender right now, I guess. I'm your man. The bar is full, and it's

early. I know Dry Martinis, Singapore Slings, anything you want. I can whip it up.

The tall DD boss's reaction was short. He sussed up the guy... what did he say his name was? Jonathan? Well, the boss was a particularly good businessman. Quick to ask, swift to make a decision.

As for Winkler, he immediately thought about the tips he could earn, even if only for one night, and compared with what he'd made in the past, well, interesting.

Play it solid, you have a chance here, little boy from rural Vermont, he thought.

— Where did you work before?
— Dozens of bars in Vermont, Chicago and in Montreal, Canada, where I was a student. And very recently too, I got back to this job, parttime, on the university campus, on busy nights. Women love me at the bar, all ages, guys too.
— Keep your answers short. How do you make a Singapore Sling?
— Original recipe uses gin, Benedictine, Cherry Heering, club soda and important, fresh pineapple juice: better from Sarawak pineapples.
— And a Pink Lady?
— Gin for 1.5 ounces, Applejack, 0.5 ounce, then 4 dashes of grenadine, the juice of a half lemon, and one with egg if desired. Shake with ice, and top with a cherry. Several versions exist. Can show you one right now.

After Winkler answered the boss's queries on the B52, the Grasshopper, the Stinger, the Herbsaint frappé, the Nuclear Martini and a couple others, made shook up the poison wannabe, the good stuff, the delicious feast for the eyes, tongue and heart, the boss tried a last question: the pitfall.

— You can make the School Binder drink?
— I don't know, or maybe it doesn't exist, as far as I'm concerned.
— Good answer, so, what about taxes?
— The machine takes care of it.
— What if a client doesn't want to pay, or delays?
— I ask again, and, if needed, politely I point to the armed security guy, right there, with a smile. I'm used to this.
— Okay, listen, wise man. You're in for the next 15 minutes. If things go okay, for the next hour, after, maybe all night, then we'll will see. If not, if things don't go smart for these first 15 minutes or so, or even before, you're out without pay, and leave the tips here. Okay?
— Deal!

Winkler ran busy all night, the boss apparently happy. Clients didn't seem to notice, except four or five of them enquiring about Billy.

There was no way of knowing at the time, but Winkler had a new job, a fantastic job in a fantastic bar, in fantastic Manhattan. The hell with his heavy diplomas, at least for now.

As the hours passed, the boss became more and more relaxed. He saw Jonathan was a pro, and smiling, and he accepted what he really now understood: he deeply needed this kind of energy.

But what Winkler didn't know, what he hadn't bargained for, was yet to come. He'd gotten so much more, including future serious trouble.

***

A few minutes before 3 in the morning, Winkler had made a fair amount of cash at the bar, closely watched by the boss.

Before he left, the manager told him he'd call him the very next day, early.

Early, got it, Winkler said, giving him something of a prudent, respectful smile.

The boss was clearly very satisfied.

— We were already missing one or two good barmen, he said.

Tips in pocket, Winkler went out into the city that never sleeps, under a heavy rain and gusty northeast winds. He didn't care. Even a glacial snow storm would not bother.

Everything about the night was totally unexpected. All. And the strange words from Billy still troubled him.

Back at his hotel room, he noticed he still had a wallet in his loose pants. Not his own. When the manager had bumped him away from Billy, Winkler fell on the ground, directly onto a small wallet. As a reflex, he had put it swiftly into his own pocket, as he always did at any other bar, whenever he happened upon a lost item.

Busy and drunk clients often left their belongings somewhere in the bar, and Jonathan was quick to spy these lost wallets but also quick to hand over the whole thing, intact, cash and bank cards still inside, to the owner, or several minutes later. He did not want trouble, never had.

Somehow, Billy had dropped his own, possibly while collapsing, a huge point for Jonathan's future.

In the black purse, Jonathan found $4,000 US, 2,000 Euros, $540 Canadian, 820 British pounds, various other less known currencies, and a little, apparently inoffensive, red USB key.

At home, not tired in the least, he went immediately to his computer and plugged in the key, about to copy the contents in his own computer.

But it was password protected. He intended to return the money to Billy, but, remembering the talks about Prince Marty the Third, he suspected it could be risky to do this.

"Damned if you do, damned if you don't," he said out loud to no one in particular. Maybe the "don't" was the lesser evil, so he kept the money and the colorful USB key, at least he'd keep it for a moment.

There were 40 gigs on it, so a reasonably large amount of information could be stored there.

After some messy trials, Jonathan found a tricky way to open files, on the web, with a free algorithm to unlock easy passwords. He had good contacts at Vermont U. Open sesame: the key was about to deliver its secrets.

There it was: a list of names from an Excel file. And plenty of information about each name: date of birth, profession, nationality, estimated revenue, function, strengths, weaknesses, some attached photos, and plenty of strange explanatory notes. Then, one more column called "Risk."

What the hell was all this... for a bartender?

Jonathan looked attentively at the list, even if it was very late, around 4:15 in the morning. Even if he had woken up at 5 the day before, driven to New York from Burlington, taken a drink before Billy's collapse. And even if he had ended up with a new terrible job in the heart of the Big Apple, the heart of the planet, says the New Yorker.

10,205 Excel lines. 10,205 names. All nationalities under the sun.

A good calculator, Jonathan estimated: that's what was needed: 25 years of work for Billy, and, this would be, what? Around 400 names a year? Say, 250 days of work per year, one or two names per day of work?

Yeah, it was plausible. But why? What was the link with Prince Marty, the Third? What was the last word from Billy? "Rev"? A revolver, a revolt, a political revolving door? Or did it only mean "revoke," as in "to revoke something"? Or had Billy just uttered a word, very weakly, that meant nothing at all?

On the list, information was often missing. For example, for many names, Billy did not enter the profession, nor the year of birth or age, nor the strengths. But the estimated legal and illegal approximate revenues or wealth was almost always noted.

Still, why this file?

Jonathan's mind was busy running circles around the same points. In his recent Masters courses on International

Economics, one of his teachers had suspected that the real impact of the international mafia and of "white collar crimes" was way underestimated, even hidden or half intentionally ignored by the press, politicians, historians, and economists.

This professor clearly said some of them lived with the pressure not to talk or were paid to write false or misleading claims or to write only on more... well, more benign subjects. Though Jonathan was not totally sure of the importance of that teacher's ideas, he was freaking out a bit with Billy's list now in hand.

The 10 first names were totally unknown to him. Certainly not to Billy. But not without interest.

The list looked like this.

- Mark Dusk. Surname: Murky. Date of birth: October 31, 1960. International trader of all goods in all countries. Bachelors in Engineering at Louisiana Tech University. Graduated 1983. Might always have a gun on him. Loves blonde women with big breasts. VD.
- Oleg Kulagin, born September 1954. Surname: Kee-Oleg. Russian émigré, billionaire. Former Gas-Prone Executive. Past life: unknown, KGB/FSB (Russian secret services) not excluded. His grandfather Boris was a member of the Okhrana, the ex-secret police of the last Tsar Nicolas II, until 1917. Officially killed in 1918 by the Bolsheviks, but in fact by Stalin's guys in the 1930s purges. Immensely rich, with several Swiss Banks accounts. Last visit to the DD: October 15th

2007. Estimated income in 2008: 140 million US $. (source: NY Times, The Guardian UK, and some talks with him). Wealth: minimum $50 million. VD.

- Henri Chaux: Surname: Chaud-Chaud, meaning Hot-Hot. French international soccer player. Date of birth: July 22nd, 1978. Suspected of having arranged some results in international soccer games, as he's top goalkeeper, the only top goalkeeper able to play forward on a regular basis. Perhaps threatened by the Russian mafia, has a lot of affairs with Russians and other young women; some are spies. Revenues 2008: published, 7 million Euros. ND.
- Paul O'Donohue: British and Canadian businessman. Income: around $20 million, in 2008, probably, very subjective. Has all kinds of top government, United Nations, European Union connections. Was a major UK political organizer, working behind the scenes. D?
- Leslie Warn: Former Yale student in Law. Year of birth: 1982. Nice blonde. Favorite of Chaux, and of others. Revenue: as a saleswoman at Macy's, probably $55,000 US declared. Much more undeclared, looking into the expenses she made at the DD. ND.

Jonathan sorted them, in Excel, by alphabetic order.

With a dramatic smile and AAAHHH!, he noted more than ten princes in the list, and Marty the Third was one of them.

At 6 a.m., as he was about to go to bed, the boss at the DD called. Apparently, he'd been very enticed by Jonathan's quickness, friendliness, exact counts, and general work. He offered to meet at a coffee shop close to the Empire State Building. At 9, and discuss pay, hours, days, clients, other barmaids, all things Jonathan knew reasonably well.

So, what could he say but yes, knowing he would be busy behind the DD bar very soon.

With that, Jonathan fell fast asleep.

Jonathan's Youth

A Modest Family

1962 was a year full of important events. It was the year Jonathan was born.

When Billy had collapsed at the DD, in June 2010, Jonathan was 48. So, he did not, could not remember the John F. Kennedy assassination in Dallas in 63, but clearly he could remember 68, the year of a few other striking killings: namely, JFK's brother Robert's in Los Angeles and Martin Luther King's in Tennessee.

Between the ages of twelve and sixteen, Jonathan had read much on both brothers and on the preacher from Georgia. And on the riots, people's skin torn right off their bones, by the sharp, bared teeth of dogs, all this from some used books and magazines donated by the local charity association.

He'd dipped his nose in the pages on the strange conclusions of the Warren Commission, Lyndon Baines Johnson taking over after JFK and on the Vietnam war.

But in his neck of the world in little Richford, Vermont, Jonathan had found too few friends to discuss all this with, aside from one of his three sisters, Jane, who was equally captivated with such events.

The family house was an old one, built around 1845: a two floor-cottage, small, a bit cold in winter, though the woodstove made a good job of it. But it was hot in summer, as insulation was basic, and of course no air conditioning.

The second floor was particularly hot some days in July and August. A small 25 feet by 25 feet structure. You could get underneath through a trap in the center of the house, into a storage area built into the ground, where potatoes and other vegetables were warehoused during winter.

Winter was long and cold in northern Vermont, but the wind not too much a factor because of the location of the house in the mountains. Chilly wind was welcome in summer, hated in winter.

The house was four miles from the village, rural, isolated, quiet, with ten children. A brook was going through their own small woodland, half a mile behind the house, ending in a bigger river, the Missisquoi River, a tributary of the Yamaska River in Canada, ultimately pouring into the Atlantic Ocean through the Quebec province's huge St-Lawrence River.

The wood and brook surroundings were a place to take walks and relax, hear bird songs and sometimes see a coyote, a bobcat or their prey, rabbits and deer.

The house was simply furnished. No luxury, very basic, black and white TV until 1973. Only one bathroom. But a surprising quantity of books, of many kinds. Including a significant proportion on history, international politics, wars, and about the UN, the World Bank, and other international organizations. Comics and much more.

Meals were very good, thanks to the rural space available for agriculture, so plenty of vegetables, and rather cheap local meat.

Carrots, beets, beans, corn, potatoes, cucumbers, tomatoes, and even many local fruits were there for the picking, strawberries, blackberries and cherries, and specialty apples from Vermont orchards and the ones from up in Quebec, north of the border, less than 10 miles away. Or using the international metric system, less than 15 kilometers away. Jonathan used both systems, interchangeably.

Mother was a fine cook. She enjoyed variety in the day to day, avoiding routine and lovely yelling from the children about it. "It's ready!" she would shout, smiling. The little army charged then.

Dessert was less frequent but not absent and not bad when it was laid out in. Cakes, pies, ice cream, and some Jell-O when mom had no time. Jonathan knew sugar and other luxury food often came from third world countries, not as rich as they were in Vermont, and it was a comparison because he knew they weren't really. Rich, that is: the Winkler family wasn't. And the same metrics on sugar could be used when considering oil and gas, and more.

His room was shared with his oldest brother and was arranged with basic furniture, the bed and mattress not too comfortable. The family budget was restrictive, goods limited. So was the general comfort of most rooms, except for the kitchen, with the beautiful oak table that Jonathan's father had built from a big tree sacrifice.

The house was not insured, nor was the car, until the mandatory car insurance law came into force sometime in

74 or so. First things first, said Father. Insurance, second. Or third. Or even lower down the rung.

But Jonathan didn't complain about anything. Usually, after a long day of physical work in the crop fields or playing the various sports he loved, such as baseball, football or even hockey with old balls and home-made pucks from whatever piece of rubber or other available material they had under hand, sleep was not long to come, quality bed or not. He enjoyed a happy childhood.

Teddy, who was simply named not for the teddy bear itself but for Theodore Roosevelt, was his companion. "Teddy," because Jonathan's grandfather often talked about the first Roosevelt president.

Grandpa was born in 1889 and was a fan of Teddy R., even if he thought the USS Maine explosion in the Havana harbor in 1898, starting the US war against Spain, was a little disgraceful on the part of the 26th president of the US. His uncles believed this ship explosion had been a provocation by the US, by its army generals. To influence the public opinion at the time and to justify the war against Spain. Jonathan's father was unsure, but discussions sometimes were ignited when Jonathan showed up with the little bear.

At the Richford local school, teachers were not always as qualified as they should have been to teach the precocious and not so precocious, but what they really wanted was success for their students. Jonathan liked them: locals, dedicated, and rarely missing a day. He would never forget them, and Mother and Dad respected them.

It was one such teacher, Ms. Laura, who, in his fourth grade, encouraged Jo to read a lot, so that when he was eleven, he really took off and read all the magazines and books he could find, enjoying history, geography and much more.

His childhood bicycle had large tires, sort of like today's mountain bikes, and it was cherished. Five speeds. So, with the hilly, dusty roads all around, Jonathan developed muscular legs and calves.

He rode to his aunt's house quite often, for a few molasses cookies and to talk about things academic and sometimes politics. Her place was four miles away, on a difficult, dirt, narrow, but how beautiful it was, roller-coaster road.

In 2010, unimaginably, Jo still had this bike with wooden pedals and smooth springs under the seat. He'd kept it in good working order and loved it. He had adapted it, welding here and there, to his adult height. He used it in Manhattan, even, sometimes bringing it on the back of his car for lovely journeys to the countryside or, on occasion, to Canada.

In front of his childhood house was a dirt road, dirt around the house and a lot of dirt roads in the surrounding area. They poured asphalt down on some of them in the region many years later. When Jonathan left home at 18, there were still ochre routes in most of his county. But, for him, this was a kind of protected paradise for cycling. The rural paths were surprisingly well drained, so the rain didn't stay for long.

He did not want to have "his" much-loved dirt roads, what he called his personal playing field, asphalted and widened. Manhattan was an asphalt world, a motorized world, a business world, but it would reveal for him a kind of dirty world often, but awesome in other ways.

Sadly, Jonathan was not to be happier, in the heart of the Windy City than on the dirt roads of his youth, biking around. And not as safe. Not exactly unsafe, but, well, dirt roads, in short, underneath the sure rubber of a bicycle wheel were far safer than Chicago, or NY. Simple men and women are happy when they stay with their little things, or when the powerful ones let them live quietly with their little things, in their little homes, wrote some unknown author. These half-red, half-brown rural ways were his "little things," even if he were in his late 40s.

When he was growing up, the neighbor's girl, Julia, was cute, brilliant and funny. She was one year younger, and they always played together: biking together, playing board games like Monopoly, backgammon, crosswords, Payday, cards, dice, Pig in the Garden, hopscotch, and so many other.

But in the early 70s, on her bike, not two miles away from her home, she was hit by a small pickup truck passing far too fast. The driver was drunk, very drunk in fact, but the law was weak in Vermont and all across the US and Canada during those years.

The guy was never convicted. He'd even left the scene of the accident, leaving his vehicle to run into the woods, supposedly trying to get help from the closest house he expected to find over the hill. Little Julia died on site, alone, from the injuries and from blood loss. The driver came back four hours later, sufficiently sober.

Jonathan read, years after, that car accidents today are still a main cause of death, if not *the* main cause of death, for people under 30, according to respected actuarial sources of information.

Jo's mother

Anita was born in 1934, the third daughter and fifth child of eleven children. Not really poor, but certainly not wealthy. Two other brothers were stillborn.

She witnessed World War II, from a teenager's eyes. Adolf Hitler, Hermann Goering, the Gestapo, the SS in Germany and Mussolini's gang in Italy, and other similar guys forever scared her. She did not want, at any cost, to send her boys into any war. Her grandmother often talked about the 1900 war in South Africa, the Boer's war. She said that war was only for diamonds.

Diamonds! They did not have any.

Were they less happy, Jonathan's mother reasoned with her daughters and sons. No, not at all. No diamonds, no BMWs, not much cash, but happy. Don't let yourself be squeezed into a pitfall by a richer man, she told her children. If he does not have a heart, girls were told, he's not worth your love.

Jonathan's grandma was born in 1900 and died in 1970, from a heart attack, during the Vietnam war. She said, when she was in her last days, that this war disgusted her and would kill her. So many disgraceful scenes on the television, on a daily basis. Who wasn't to see it?

How to understand how much manpower could be spent, hundreds of billions of dollars, all to kill each other.

And knowing that arms merchants were selling to both side of the fence… billions taken from honest US taxpayers!

"War profiteering" was popular, and even respected, according to her. Billions of dollars when they were not able, in their own community, the "village," they called it, to establish a public library.

Because the mayor, the state governor and the two senators said it would cost too much.

Less than $200 to start it with a reasonable quantity of books, she said, in 1890. Teachers were, according to her, very badly paid, but many big war firms made huge, huge profits every year during the Vietnam war.

Mom Anita boarded a plane for the first time in 1989, thanks to daughter Ginette and her regular salary at the local bank in Richford. Anita and Ginette went to the Rockies and Utah. Zion Park and Bryce Canyon were her favorites.

Literate, mainly on her own, but partly because a generous donor permitted Anita to go to more advanced studies. But still far from university. Then she was an elementary school teacher a few years, in a rural school in northern Vermont, and showed her own children.

Private donors were a kind of precursor of the public state loans system for those wishing to study. Some requested interest, at low or very low rates; a lot did not. Anita had read before about marvelous Utah's scenes; that's why she wanted to go.

She was not wrong. Zion's fall colors were unforgettable. Butch Cassidy, hiding around Zion, and other bandits of this style were well known to her. On one of the walls of the small house, a large photo was often looked at, and made the family immortalize these wonderful days.

She loved children, but died, not from a gun, but from that dirty lung cancer at 57. She never smoked, but manipulating chemical products in the garden without gloves could have been harmful. No one would ever know.

She often phoned Jonathan when he was studying Economics at Burlington University, 55 miles southwest from Richford. Jonathan never said he would leave Vermont after, but never said he would stay.

They talked about his last exam percentage, the group's average on this particular test, and would he be okay to finish his course on time and on target with good grades.

Sometimes about girls. I know you may want to have fun, but protect yourself from bad relationships, she said. One thing Jo never explained to himself: too often, when he was about to call Mom Anita, the phone rang in his small student room, and it was her. He did not believe in parapsychology, but so many times was strange, unexplained.

When he was off for a weekend and back in Northern Vermont, in Richford, the rest of the family usually, and almost always, came on Sunday afternoon to visit Mom and Dad. To chat, have a beer, play cards and other board games, make crosswords, play chess, have a good time.

They all ate at Mom's home for dinner, discussing politics with Dad, sometimes intentionally making him half-mad (and it was not so hard to do!). JFK's assassination was often back on the table, but Robert's one did hurt Dad even more. Not one but two! In the face of the whole world. Bang! Bang! And the strange Warren commission conclusions…

These family's meeting were happy times, but not all the children were there every week. Normally, say, half of them would come for a visit, not the same ones each time. So, they all kept in contact. Connected to Vermont.

Sometimes a new boyfriend or girlfriend came in, or a wannabe. He or she was the "turkey stuffing" and was on the receiving end of many jokes, a warm welcome to the family. How long will you "stay"? Will you be "better" for us than the previous one? Do you really love her? Are you thinking of staying together, as they were speaking to Jonathan or one of his brothers. And so on.

Mother used to say like this: You, my children, do not know hunger. I do. My father, in particular, really did, she was saying, once in a while.

You're so lucky to live in these richer years now, and not in these big towns where criminality is so high. She went to the mass, but Father Ernest was not too convinced.

Jo's dad

Father Ernest was born in 1931, a bit stocky with big, powerful hands.

Strong enough to put down the two little bad guys in Richford when they were drunk, Benny and Michael Greenwood, both at the same time, without really hurting them. Honest workers, but harsh guys when drinking. They used to be very friendly, until more and more alcohol modified their reactions and brought on horrible behavior, as well as an ugly and not so false reputation.

Ernest liked baseball as well as hockey. He played hockey sometimes, with the boys, on their own little pond he had created by blocking the brook between the small hills in front of the house, about 500 feet to the left of the 1890s gray, wood barns.

He once went to a Montreal Canadians game in the Montreal Forum up in Canada.

It was closer than Boston, although he was a moderate Big Bad Boston Bruins fan. In fact, he did like professional sports. But sliding to the end of his life, when average salaries of these stars became more than ten times higher the median income of hard workers like him, he became a little disgusted and no longer understood the fascination these athletes generated.

The country's situation, and politics, were often a subject for discussion. Republicans, Democrats, the Kennedys, Vietnam, World War I and II, Lenin, Stalin, the Quebec case next door, a few miles away north of the border, US presidents, Vermont Governors and Senators, Richford and Montpelier mayors, Quebec and Canadian prime ministers including Lester B. Pearson, who won a Nobel Peace prize, you name it.

Discussion had the goal of provoking the discussion itself, first, kind of "win" the discussion, second, and simply have fun, third.

Ernest was not active as such in politics, though he participated in one commission on education in the 60s. Government wanted, he said, to have several uneducated guys on it. Even if they did not admit it officially. He said he was not even able to speak enough to be considered. Experienced bureaucrats sitting on the commission took all the place. Decisions were taken in advance, in the corridors, the days and weeks before the meetings. Which sometimes were a mere facade, according to him.

When he talked about this commission, he mumbled more than explained, but his general idea was clear for his children: their findings were almost all set before it started, and guys like him did not have any big words. The government officials merely wanted to have uneducated guys and women, not to listen to them, but to "save the face," look good, and build political capital for the next election.

Anita was not agreeing. She mentioned a lot of elements on which Ernest, according to her, had had an influence on the result.

Since he was not educated and had no diploma to earn from a single "real" job, from his own terminology, Ernest had many sources of income: the farm, school buses he rode a few years, winter shovels for removing the road snow, real estate agent (he took a good crash course for it, a "crush course," as he joked).

He was quite brilliant. After getting rid of the farm ill animals, he sold many properties in the 1970s as a real estate broker, also buying, selling and renting some other goods, a few machines, like small tractors and light machinery, lawn mowers, for instance.

He liked to say, the progressive income tax system is great, and a government from the center too, but if all the mob pays 100% of their income tax, I will too.

Jonathan was used to being questioned by dad. Good questions. And tricky ones. What will you study at college, and even university? Will you apply it? How will it be useful to society and to you? Will you be paid by my taxes, working for the State or the State Hydro Company, doing almost nothing on Fridays? he smiled.

Discussions between Ernest and JP, his friend and a local teacher, on all these subjects, were succulent and really funny. JP would play devil's advocate. Ernest knew this and played along, sometimes forgetting JP did it intentionally; so, he'd get a little mad, particularly about the unseemly high salaries of bureaucrats, governors, senators and the trolley of their "handy helpers," as he called them.

Jonathan often joined in as a middleman, arbitrator, or taking JP's side for more fun. Insurance, too, was a mad-at-it subject for Ernest.

Insurance? I can't even afford a new coat every year, so how the hell could I buy insurance? These companies return only 5 cents a dollar of premiums they receive to clients on claims, Ernest would say. Indeed, it was not true Ernest could not buy a new coat, but he was really questioning the real value of insurance. And his house was indeed insured, Ernest good friend and cousin John being his insurance broker, though Ernest sometimes said it was not, only for sparkling a discussion.

— 5 percent? Hum, start your own insurance company, man, start your own, now, JP urged him.

They often played cards, with some very local home games, often unknown 30 miles away, having been transmitted father to son, and mother to children. The "beef" game, the best card game according to Ernest and his boys, was a real nice one that all the Winklers played.

The Winklers had made it a kind of a protected, family game, carefully choosing who was about to learn the rules and tricks. A new boyfriend was not allowed to play until, at least, he'd been with one of the Winkler's daughters several months, and surely not to good hints if the relationship hadn't lasted a few years. The "beef cards game" was THE "beef game," in this rural family.

Every single day, Jonathan was, somehow, going back to his roots when confronted to a new difficult situation. He had heavily traveled across almost all US states, cruised in several Canadian provinces and abroad, in Europe, South America and more, had worked in the highest floors of the highest Chicago's and Boston's buildings, but on many aspects, he was still a little guy from sympathetic Northern Vermont.

And Mom liked to say he was still in his 20s, as for his behavior.

Murky Guys at the Bar

Winkler was working at the DD bar on that Saturday night, June 5th, 2010.

The regular crowd started to shuffle in and more heavily around 9 pm.

Young ladies, usually nicer than not: this was an upper-class Manhattan bar. They sometimes, of course, cruised Jonathan, and he played the game. As JP had with his father, when the girls had discussions in front of him.

As a bartender in Vermont and in Quebec, he was often invited to a private party afterward. The francophones from Quebec he knew were particularly funny and enjoyed parties. But they were hard workers, too, and successful when studying. He'd had several good friends from Montreal.

Young guys were there too at the DD. Middle aged men as well, at times fathers and sons, mothers and daughters, some sports groups, more often political or citizens groups, and, of course, heavyweight bureaucrats and diplomats. A lot of businessmen. Also, unavoidably, your typical lonely man, lonely woman, at times leaving together after a while, hand in hand. Various nationalities was the rule, as was the case that evening.

Around 7:15 pm, four guys went in. Three who were strong, tall and rough, and a fourth, much smaller and thinner, came in and asked for a very specific table. Jo saw them pointing at the only table in a little corner of the DD that had a kind of Catholic church rood screen against it, a few feet above the other tables, the wall behind it.

They seemed to be used to the place.

The smaller one looked like a lawyer, very different from the three others. Jo rushed over, right after the hostess had left them. Three Blue Moon beers and one complex version of a Miami Latino cocktail, this one for the small man, who did all the ordering. He had no clear accent, Jo noticed, but the three other ones had strong southern way to speak.

At least one of them was from somewhere in the Texas panhandle, probably. Winkler was a pro at accents, he loved it.

Soon, many people came to the tables situated "beneath" the rood screen, as Jo started to call it. He strode back to the bar, glancing back once. Who knew why, but something about that table and the guys looked bizarre. Three rough guys, with a lot of tattoos, one dandy, as he called him.

He watched them while preparing the Miami shot, but the whole team seemed to be silent. Maybe more than a bit odd. Jonathan brought over the beers and the Latino cocktail; then he was called by another table, on a lower level, filled by four very nice-looking Turkish women in their late twenties, maybe early thirties.

As soon as he got there, the rough guys called him not very loudly for a second beer.

Jo made sure he was not showing he understood, to be polite for the women. He was single, too. Service was important! He was in fact very surprised. The guys on high were being heard by Jonathan rather clearly but only when he was standing not far from the lower table, speaking to the women.

Strange acoustics, he thought: *kind of a Greek theater effect, perhaps.*

The four men were gesticulating above to get him to come back for more drinks. They'd finished their firsts already, and one of the pretty, young women at this table made a sign to the guys with a hand on her right ear.

They lifted their beers and pointed them toward the table of women, to Jonathan.

He glanced up, put his hand to his ear, too, then raised his index finger. One minute please, gentlemen, I will get to you.

The guys certainly thought they would not be listened to. Jo's capacity for hearing was fine. Usually, he didn't enjoy too much noise and made sure that at his favorite place at the bar, not too far from the cash, the noise level was acceptable. Otherwise, he'd simply get up and make another corner of the bar his part-time home for a minute. But while taking the order from these women, what he clearly heard from the table on the higher level frightened him.

He tried to keep up his smile for the women and to the one in particular who was showing a rather clear interest, he flashed a gentle smile. All the while taking down the orders from these beautiful sirens, noticing he could hear better what was being said from the table on high if he was at a very precise spot. Ah, acoustics.

— The bartender and clients clearly cannot hear us from there, so who needs to speak?, the small one was saying.
— So, let's talk quickly then, said one of the three, who had a Texas drawl. Business as usual? New things? Big money, oil, gold, diamonds, bauxite, silver, women, or what else?
— Yep, why are we here, I want to know that quickly, a second one asked, his more of what they'd call a Tennessee Grand Ole Opry accent.

Jonathan knew both these accents, as he'd biked around there, and he was kind of genius, if he did say so himself, at accents.

— I don't want to lose my Saturday night, Gerry, you know.
— All right, all right, said the third, a red-haired guy with a Vermont accent, who had joined them. We'll figure this out, then have a few more beers.

The small red-haired man looked a bit familiar to Jonathan. He kept talking, and Jo inched a little to his left to hear him better.

— Piles of light arms, guns, long and short, bombs, grenades, miniature tanks, all from the former USSR, stuff's still waiting for us in Russia, in at least ten spots. But we know the main big one's there, for sure. Well preserved, some underground, sealed; even the president and his top FSB Russian secret police are probably not aware that stash is there, and if they're aware at all only think that there's not much of it.

The guys were religiously listening.

— Don't ask me how come I know this. But we have to be quick. Prince Marty the Third wants to buy it from us, resell at a price 20 times higher, or more who knows... we pay the key guys, including the few guys with the warehouse keys. Or get rid of them. We secure the transport all the way. We keep 10%, as usual; no one sees it, as usual too.
— Who knows about this, who contacted you?, one said.
— The Armando Company, from Luxemburg. They apparently heard about it from one of Joseph Stalin's illegitimate great grandsons, confirmed to me by a Canadian mafioso, a Russian émigré, and a well-known professor at Cornell University. Armando sold all kinds of luxury goods to the former USSR top Politburo women and men: evening dress fashion, fine alcohol and wines, cigars, perfume, sex toys, cocaine, gold, jewels, Modigliani's, Stradivarius... they still do smuggling in many countries.
— What's a Modigliani?, the Texan asked.
— What's the Politburo?, the Tennessee one asked. The small dandy man politely answered.
— Modigliani is a famous painter, and his masterpieces are worth many hundreds of

thousands of dollars each, some more. The Politburo was the top of the top executives of the USSR machine, Stalin, Beria, Khrushchev, Trotsky, Molotov… C'mon, wake up. Armando's machine, still very active today, only two guys know in fact, discretely made the contact, and all is ready to go.

— You have to secure enough trucks and a safe route from Smolensk to Arkhangelsk on the White Sea, or on any easy sea with a friendly port. Then some boats, but, first, is the Smolensk place, where is the warehouse, and bring trucks.
— What about the Russian watch at the warehouse site and all around there?
— At the warehouse, Armando brains have already secured it.
— But on the roads?
— Weak safety, Daniel. We know the fellow Chechen mobs, and we have to pay them in stages. Rather easy, I think.
— A few million, of course?
— No.
— No?
— This time, a few billion… in total, maybe several separate operations to come.
— Billion?
— Yes. May be up to two billion. Would be several jobs, the first one for several hundred million.
— Dangerous?
— Dangerous? You bet. But listen, 10% is 200 million US for the whole job. Much more than your regular

assignments, and to pay your own parts, we will discuss. But we'll make it, if you're interested, that is. Even if you're not, you're already at risk by knowing about the thing, guys. So, what'll it be? Then, you ARE interested... no question.

Jonathan had heard enough; what's more, he'd already been standing at this table way too long. A lot of clients were waiting for him. Even if he was not the only bartender, he was one of the main. Was risky to listen, while talking to the four beauties? No, probably the rough guys would be thinking: the babes are so cute, bartender's wise to chat. The music, for its part, was loud enough, so they couldn't possibly think he was listening in.

Twenty seconds later, Jonathan was at their table.

— Not easy to hear us down there?
— Yep, hard to do. Hand signs work better!
— You took an eternity! But with those beauties, we would've done the same. Bring us four Budweiser and four double Kentucky Jim Beam Bourbon whiskeys on the rocks, ASAP.
— Okay guys. Sorry about the girls. (Jonathan winked.) I'll be right back with your order. So, do you know who the Bourbons were? he said, taking the empty bottles and glasses.
— No, the rough ones said in unison.
— Yeah, said the smaller guy. The longest dynasty of French kings, the last ones, both guillotined in 1789: Louis XVI along with his wife, the unforgettable Marie-Antoinette.

- How was the guillotine working, exactly? asked the Texan.
- A kind of a huge knife; name comes from its inventor, Guillot. It cuts off a person's head in one blow, comes down from high above. It was a kind of new, civilized serial killing. Extensively used during the French revolution, between 1789 and 1799. And the Nazis may have used it, by the way, here and there, for the ones who wouldn't salute, I mean, pledge allegiance to Hitler and the Nazi Party.

This small man was not bad at history. Not bad at all. A wealthy, high-level, educated crook?

- Better than being burned or undergoing death in Ivan the Terrible's hands, in Russia, though, said Jonathan.
- Who is this Yvan? asked the Tennessee guy. Where's he live?
- Relax, he's not the boss of Gas-Prone. Yvan was a Russian tsar.
- I know Gas-Prone. Many Russian stars, but not this terrible Yvan.
- I know you know Gas-Prone, the Russian natural gas and energy giant. Who doesn't? But we're not talking about a _star_. It's a _tsar_. Tsar Yvan died in Moscow in 1478, or maybe in the Chechen capital, Grozny, meaning "The Terrible," as in Yvan's nickname.

But Jonathan was already making his way back to the bar and, although very perplexed, laughing a bit inside. What a mystery… the ex-USSR, arms, Gas-Prone, Gerry the redhead—maybe he knew him? So, what else would there be? He shook his head in disbelief.

Passing a small table, he heard two drunk guys singing, "Games without Frontiers, War without Tears," the 1980s Peter Gabriel classic war song. Pure coincidence, probably.

***

At $2,000 a night, for 250 days, he would earn $500,000 a year… but, not every evening was a Friday or Saturday, and this one was probably a profitable one. Anyways, he had to find out soon what the income tax rates on tips were and to discuss with his father his comments on "the progressive income tax system," Ernest says "great, but if and when all the mob's paying its due income tax, I'll pay all my own too." And he'd have to put aside money for these income taxes at the end of the year, now.

At home, sitting on his couch, munching on chips, Jonathan was unable to sleep. He mulled over what he'd heard, was still astonished over the last hour or so at the DD, overhearing what those guys were saying.

As he was going over the conversation, thinking about his taxes, he decided to donate a part of his pay to Oxfam, to UNICEF, Doctors Without Borders, or to other respectable, not-for-profit local, national, or international relief organizations. He would do it as soon as he could, maybe directing it toward children living in poverty. He didn't have any kids, so this would be his own contribution, in a way. He quickly looked at Billy's list, having closed the Internet on his laptop computer and deleted all cookies and other traces of the sites he went on. Prudence, he told to himself.

He flipped through the listing, all 10,205 names, sorted by first name. Then, he snuck a peek, and searched for any Daniel or, maybe, Dan?

A Daniel Liddy was the one he found.

Billy knew him well apparently, as his entry was full of notes on him on the Excel line. Photo included. No doubt, this was the Daniel who was at the DD.

Born in 1956 in Nashville, Tennessee. Son of a welder from the Teamster's and a stay-at-home mother. Stopped studying at 15, did various jobs, including murky ones. Indicted for cocaine traffic in Nashville in September 2000. (Billy had included a newspaper article on him and this conviction.) Nothing since. Estimated revenue: declared $50,000; undeclared: more than $600,000, maybe much more. Last DD visit: August 2006. D.

Then there was Gerry, the redhead. Could he be any more difficult to find? Jonathan was quite sure he was from Vermont. So, he sorted the list by state.

Yes! Here it was.

Gerard O'Connor! Now he remembered the red-haired guy. *A small, small world,* Jo thought. He would add some info about him to Billy's list. Born around 1955, sometimes coming into the Richford post office, where Jonathan, very young, hanged around from time to time. His father was unknown, but Jonathan knew the mother: a well-dressed and haired single lady working at the Senator's office in

Montpelier, Vermont, as a clerk or on some such job, often back in Richford on weekends.

He remembered hearing her say to the red-haired man, her son, who were waiting in line, "Gerry, you'll never go anywhere waking up at noon and with your room being such a nightmare."

Billy's list had Gerry's estimated revenue: unknown, probably around $40,000, declared, and sure $1,000,000+ undeclared. Residence: 234, Chester Arthur Road, in Bordoville, Vermont! Very close to Richford, Jonathan's birthplace!

Jonathan had biked there last year. A nice, hilly road, asphalted from Duffy Hill Road to the old Chester Arthur house, then a narrow, hilly-curvy dirt road toward Bordoville. The red route was probably in the same state as it was during Chester Arthur's youth and presidency in 1881–1885. He was not elected, as he served as Vice President and replaced James Garfield, the assassinated president. Arthur was not re-elected.

Gerry redhead's residence was one mile from this house, still a national monument in Vermont, and 15 miles southwest of Richford. Only one employee was usually on site, in the tiny house for a former president. It was in fact quite similar to Jonathan family's house. Yep, a small, small world, Jonathan thought again and again.

Now for the Texan, something, Billy? Fifty guys on the list were from Texas. No match, apparently, no match. And no photo to help. Nothing. Jonathan started on the 10,206th Texan name on the list.

He saw that 9,200 were men and only a little over 1,000 or so were women. Estimated revenue for the Texan: if he wanted to respect Billy's rules, he had to find one, so he gave them the same amount as for Gerry, $50,000, and wrote "undeclared", obviously. But why was it important to Billy?

Jonathan had, indeed, given back Billy's wallet to the police the following day and took none of his cards. He kept the USB key and the money, as he suspected the police could reach out to him again because of the content, or they'd harass Billy. If he gets better... Jo may give him back his money. May. The police had told him Billy was in a coma.

***

Sunday, June 6th, 5 a.m.

The City of Smolensk, in Russia. Jonathan wanted to know more about this place the outlaws had talked about.

Wikipedia was a logical choice, although Jonathan had an old book on Smolensk from the Harvard University Press, written in 1958. *Smolensk under Soviet Rule.* He'd bought it for $2 on Boylston Street in Boston, in a used book factory, while walking around, years ago.

A secret archive from the Stalin years in the 1930s, describing the USSR system, the Trotsky Red Army, purges, the kulaks rich peasants, collectivization of the land and kolkhozes, the Communist party controls, the organs of the state security, and the like.

A pearl for Jonathan on the internal mechanisms and operating ways of the Soviet system. The archive had been left behind by the Russians when the Germans invaded Smolensk in 1942, during World War II. It was then brought to Germany, to Berlin, and found by the US army at the end of the war in 1945. Then it went to Harvard, where it was heavily studied. Smolensk and this book: a coincidence, but a nice one.

In reality, Jonathan had already read much about the former USSR and about today's Russia. He'd read about the first Varangians, who'd navigated to Kiev during the nineth to eleventh centuries for commerce, the people who were now called the Vikings, to the fall of the Berlin wall and the collapse of the USSR, to the then harsh change to the era of wild, lawless capitalism in the 1990s.

He'd read details of the iron-fist leaders' tactics. He didn't know too much about Smolensk itself but would learn quickly. He should get more about it, having heard the goings-on of the table of thugs. And he had free time to fill, being single, always being ready to dig in new things, not the kind of guy to go out often to parties.

He thought he could very soon help the police, with regards to figuring out this traffic ring of arms. But how? First, he thought he would have to get well informed in order to be credible at the FBI or other international police eyes.

Smolensk, in Russia, was located about 40 miles from the Belarus border to the west, 175 miles from the closest Ukraine border to the south, more or less 260 miles to Moscow to the northeast, and, he noted, about 2,500 miles to Paris in France, to the southwest.

But, surprisingly, the distance from Smolensk to the White Sea was much greater than to any other sea. And, once at the White Sea, the arms the bandits mentioned would be extremely far from Prince Marty the Third, who was certainly operating somewhere in Africa. Humm, not so logical, that Gerry's plan.

Jonathan was a crack at geography.

While his focus was economics in university, he was well aware of its intersection with geography, the distances between cities and along trade routes, with natural obstacles to commerce, like mountains, lakes, forests, deserts, rivers, seas, and the like.

He also knew the general rules of mob trafficking: the longer the merchandise had to travel, the more bribes had to be paid, and the higher the risk of failure and seizure by the authorities or other bandits, the higher risk of killings, injuries, along with a host of other problems.

Later, at home, unable to sleep, he made a kind of table of distances to the sea, countries to cross and clearly confirmed that, from Smolensk, the White Sea was not the most logical choice. His distance table showed data from Smolensk to a few other locations. Arkhangelsk Port, on the White Sea, was a good 760 miles (or 1200 km) travel from Smolensk. And the White Sea was frozen during the winter months.

So, he looked at several other more logical options to send arms from Smolensk, in the heart of Russia, to a Prince, somewhere in Africa. As Gerry would do.

Kaliningrad Port, on the Baltic Sea, is set in a Russian enclave: to get there, you had to go through Belarus and Lithuania, or Poland, then back into the Kaliningrad enclave, a good 420 miles or more (or at least 670 km). There, you had the Gdansk Port, Poland, on the Baltic Sea: 520 miles (or 830 km). Or Klaipeda, Lithuania, on the Baltic Sea too, through Belarus and Lithuania: 350 miles (or 560 km). Riga, the Gulf of Riga, at the mouth of this Baltic Sea. You had to go through Belarus and Latvia, which was 360 miles or so (575 km). Tallin, Estonia: to get there, had to go through Russia and Estonia, 420 miles (675 km). Odessa, Ukraine, on the Black Sea, to the south. They had to go through Russia, maybe a small portion of Belarus, then into the Ukraine: 600 miles (960 km).

Another possibility was to conduct the arms transit on the big, long, Dnieper River, by boat, though, from Smolensk to Kherson, Ukraine, not so far from Odessa. But was it easier than by truck or train? Some heavy vessels were able to navigate from Kiev, Ukraine's capital, to the south, until the Black Sea, depending on the season of the year.

Good on you, Wikipedia!, Jonathan smiled, scrolling down. Interesting.

The trip would be easy enough along the Black Sea to Istanbul, then on to the Aegean and Mediterranean Seas, to the Suez Canal toward East Africa, through the Red Sea, right? But what if it was to West Africa...?

Too many hypotheses. He tried to read the last New York Times news and Jeune Afrique, in French, as he often did. Too hard, too tired. He had to sleep. It was 6 in the morning.

But he was working much later, at 6 in the evening. Jonathan hoped the women from Turkey would be back soon; he could try to talk about the Turkish controls on the sea bordering Istanbul, but he didn't know where they worked, in what field. Probably a futile effort. Still, they were so attractive.

Why hadn't he taken their phone numbers? Stupid guy, I am, he grumbled to himself.

***

Jonathan entered the DD, at 5:40 that Sunday evening, June 6th

— Hey, Mary! How are you? he asked a waitress he had chatted with a few times.
— Fine, Jonathan, and you? What about your initial full days?
— A real pleasure, rushing, but I'll survive.
— Great! I knew from the first minutes, you'd make it. Now, you'll have to keep the pace; employee turnaround is high, here.
— Billy made it 20 years, yeah?
— Yep, but he was a kind of wild tiger in its own jungle. The second longest was a barmaid worker made it 4 years only.
— And what about you?
— Six months. I should find a real job if I want to have children, but the pay isn't bad, seeing how (here, she rubbed her fingers together), well, you know, there's the money!
— Yep, you can say that again! Pay's excellent, indeed. Hey, did you study something somewhere, or experience somewhere else?
— Yes, believe it or not, I've passed the bar! Lawyer from Omaha, but I don't want to go back. No way, no how; my mother is in Florida now, and the climate's far better, even with the hurricanes. Warmer anyhow! Though not always, because summers in Nebraska are so hot, I swear.

— How old are you, if you don't mind my asking?
— No problem. I'm twenty-six.
— So, there's still plenty of time.
— Never know, my brother died of lung cancer at thirty-two.
— Yeah, you never know. Still, you'll probably be fine. In all likelihood. Well, anyhow, have a good evening of work. I have to open my cash and start. Cheers.

Crowd's normally smaller on Sundays, the boss explained. But they were coming in earlier. People worked on Monday mornings, of course, except for the diplomats and some other "crats," as Jo's father called them: those who started in the afternoon at the United Nations and in the NY federal government offices, often because of the time zones differences around the world. Jonathan noticed, amazed, how those who'd already had several beer rounds were now staring at the empty bottles on their tables.

Jo noted their loud voices and frequent laughs. Only a few pretty women on Sundays, he noticed. Typical crowd was going to be quite different, depending on the day of the week, and this he'd see soon enough.

Around 7, a few guys came in, with Gerry the redhead leading them directly to the upper table.

New information ahead maybe! This flashed through Jonathan's brain.

Be prudent, Jo, he told himself. Smile, and do *not* show you remember yesterday, unless the redhead mentions it.

— Hi guys, how are you? What to drink, some crackers, or anything else?
— Four double Smirnoff vodkas, for these Russian guys, you know, with one Coke for me, too, the red said. And how are you tonight, young man? As in good shape as yesterday?

Jonathan gulped.

— Not bad, not bad. Thanks. I'll be right back.

Gerry the former young slacker certainly was no idiot.

He spoke clearly. With few words. To the point. He noticed Jonathan was the same bartender whom he'd seen the day before, when he'd quickly spoken to the crooks, not losing any time.

Jonathan hoped that, at the very least, Gerry wouldn't recognize him from Vermont. But there was little chance: Jo hadn't seen him for sure in the last thirty years, and he was now taller and changed so much since the post office in Richford.

But careful, man, careful, he said to himself. Billy had noted Gerry's address was in Northern Vermont, and it could still be current. And the Russian guys, big risk maybe. Promising if he could hear something. But, my God, prudence.

— Here are your vodkas, gentlemen.
— I should have said triples for the vodkas. But it's okay for now; come back in 10 minutes or less. Just check over here every so often.
— I will.

Jonathan had to find a way to have people filling the lower tables just under the church rood. He changed the settings on the air conditioner, turning it way up for two or three tables, where older ladies were sipping a coffee. Three minutes later, one of the women waved her hand. Jonathan went over.

— It's too cold, here, the seventy-year-or-so-old woman said.
— Want the opposite table, there?
— Yes. Good idea, if it's warmer, sir.
— Sure. Yes it is. Let's go. Follow the guide.

He walked along the bar. The upper guys were talking. They didn't stop when Jonathan got to the table with the ladies.

Jonathan caught a look at Gerry, who was glancing over at him, thoughtfully. Could it be that Gerry recognized him? Had he told his comrades? And about his yesterday's visit?

The red man began to talk.

Clearly, they were knee-deep in this discussion.

Jonathan could not stay as long as he had yesterday, alongside the Turkish jewels.

But he could try playing a game? Moving back and forth. Maybe the older ladies would need something adjusted, along with ice, mixers, the level of music adjusted or the kind changed, and, what a miracle it was: the church rood table was not so far from the bar.

And more, behind the bar, depending on other noise and conversations whose volume was elevated by acoustics, Jonathan could hear portions of the conversations from that table, from the bar too. But it was much clearer when he was at the lower tables, serving. He could hear who was talking, more surely, from there. Had Billy done the same?

Very strange. So, he'd better be serving to the lower tables if he wanted to hear best the conversations above, but it wasn't always absolutely necessary.

The guys were not all the same as yesterday.

— The Dnieper River in Smolensk is now totally unfrozen; it's June. And far down to the south. So, that's an option, Ukraine.
— Jo was with the old women, but listening above.
— What can I get you, ladies?
— I don't like it. Too many small boats will be needed from Smolensk to Kiev, and down after. I favor Kaliningrad, or the White Sea, said the tallest one, the one with grey hair, killer eyes, and with a light Russian accent, clearly mixed with a British one.
— And the warehouse isn't so close to the harbor in Smolensk. We have to load on trucks, unload on boats, then on bigger boats in Kiev. Heavy risks and costs at each step, the second guy said, also with a Russian accent, much more pronounced, more difficult to understand.

Jonathan was quite sure he had a gun on his right ankle, underneath loose army style green pants.

— We aren't so clear what to take, said one lady.

Ladies undecided? Fine. Jonathan slowly unfolded a drink menu list and waited a bit, performing. He'd act like he was a little bothered.

— How many men do you have available? Gerry was asking.
— Not totally sure right now. But we have to be paid per kilometer, depending on the region and country, and per number of key areas we'd have to pass, like harbors, borders, controlled bridges, and per killed guys of our own, sometimes, too, if seriously injured, though in that case we take care of them in our own fashion. But the exact number of guys? No way can we tell you now, but we'll get them. Don't worry.

The third thug had spoken, just like a machine, no affect, with an accent Jonathan couldn't at all decipher.

And there was probably a long knife fitted into his green army pants, along his right leg; Jonathan couldn't be totally certain, but he had often seen knives in small bars, when honest hunters came in for fiestas after a moose was killed and cut up in pieces. In fact, this guy's clothes looked similar, like the US army's, though of a different color than the first one's army fatigues.

Two of the ladies ordered hot chocolate, and one took a light beer.

Jonathan went to the bar for the chocolates. The Russians waved him, over, a kind of 4×2 sign, with their fingers. Jo guessed they meant four double Smirnoff vodkas. He gave them to the guys before carrying over the warm chocos, since the lower table had said they were in no hurry.

— Thanks man. You're hot! said the one with the serial-killer eyes.
— That's what we wanted, for sure, but you forgot the limes.
— Okay, but you didn't give me any clear signals for limes, Jonathan joked.
— Next time, I'll try to draw a half moon with my hand.
— Great! he smiled.

Back to the bar, and to the ladies' cocoas. Furtively, he saw Gerry opening a map, but only for 30 seconds or so, pointing to some places on it, then closing it up. Gerry handed it over to the younger man, with the undefined accent. In fact, this guy looked quite scaring.

— Here are your chocolates, ladies.
— What about the Moscow mayor? asked the one with the killer eyes.
— The Moscow mayor? Aren't we far from Moscow? And wasn't he replaced by the prime minister's order, recently?
— Replaced, officially, yes, not removed from the circuit. We have to count him, maybe. I don't know for sure. But Beresoko's agreement may be required, too.
— Isn't he in England? Or even Iceland?

- None of us should know where he is, but he's still active. Remember that. And never, never pronounce his name again, Gerry said. Call him the Great Boss, or the Great, or, simply, the Boss. His agreement is not "required" at each step, of course, but the orders come from him to me.
- Thanks, young bartender, said the oldest lady.
- But you forgot one beer.
- Sorry, there are some days, you know. Brewing it right now, Jonathan joked. I'll be back soon.

Back to the bar again, quickly grabbing a Moosehead Light, then back to the ladies' table. But he had to be there for seconds only. If not, the redhead might begin suspecting things.

He heard, though not sure of all of it, the following, something about bribes, not always really knowing who was talking.

- What's the price per mile? said one.
- Too soon to say.
- But an estimate?
- Look on Wikipedia. Just type in "Chechnyan mob rates per mile or kilometer of cocaine move."
- C'mon guys, let's be serious. Yesterday, I made a commitment to get an estimate to hand over to the boss.
- But who's he, in reality? Can you tell us more?
- Not again, guys? No questions on this, okay?
- At least $1,000 per mile. Plus, extras, you know. In Russia. Probably more in Ukraine, less in Latvia.

Much less on the sea, for sure. Depends on what's inside too. Let's call it, "a friendly price." Plus, 10% on the whole thing.
— No, not 10%, not this time, and you may not be aware of the contents. For example, from Smolensk to Gdansk, Poland, 500 miles at $1,000 US each, we would pay $500,000. That's it, that's all, for all the stuff?
— It's 520 miles I think. But possibly 500. Plus, checkpoints at the border, bridges, etc., etc. And possibly more, since we don't know the content. Max, 8 trucks, 45 feet for each container. Any more trucks, and it could become unmanageable.
— Yes, so we know we won't know the content. Can you attach two containers, both together, to each truck?
— Only one, roads are too winding at places. So, I know that you know you'll pay more, maybe 20% more, we need more details soon.
— Okay, that's a fair estimate.
— But an approximation only. As honest as I can be.
— And by air?
— No. Too heavy a load, and the Smolensk airport is Gruyere cheese. And too foggy, too often.
— So, I think it's best to take this estimate.
— Yep. And let's have some more vodka. I'm tired of discussing. Bartender!

Jonathan was still at the old-hesitating-ladies' table and made as if he didn't understand the call. He went back to the bar. The Russians waved and yelled. He acquiesced and returned to them.

He noticed all these composures, in order to a search in Billy's database.

The rest of the evening went smoothly, although a good group of "somecrats" from Africa, probably Senegal, more than solidly tipped.

Two other quiet men did tip normally, took only Perrier, and looked very serious. Jonathan recognized one Iowa politician, one from the photos on Billy's list. Talking with two pretty young women, throwing in cognacs.

Two old friends came and asked for a chess set. They took several beers, played two games, talking about their children, the war in Iraq, the BlackWaister private security firm presence there, the execution of Saddam Hussein, and about how oil and gas were dominating the world economy and managing people's day-to-day lives. Jonathan engaged in some banter, did some joking with them.

He closed the bar at 2 a.m., when it was empty.

Back at his apartment, at 2:15, he decided to sleep. Impossible. The Chechens!

Chechnya had among the most dangerous gangs in the world. Their country had been devastated by wars. During the Yeltsin era in Russia, they assured "protection" to rich new businessmen in Russia, and during 1993, the Al-Capone-year in Russia. Indeed, during 1993, there were a great number of murders, cars exploding, particularly in Moscow, in a savage capitalist struggle between a handful of oligarchs, extremely rich, and careless about societal changes that were occurring at an extraordinary quick pace in Russia, on the ashes of the recently dead USSR.

One hundred million people somehow in the Soviet middle class were thrown into dire poverty in the early 1990s. Jonathan remembered several key socio-economic indicators he'd studied during his Masters. Russia's annual GDP shrank, in four years, by about 50% and, on a per capita basis, Russia became poorer than many of South America's poorest countries. But black markets were flourishing, and a handful of billionaires were suddenly born.

New Russia's, or still the USSR's, key assets, like Gas-Prone, were sold out for a tiny fraction of their worth, to these oligarchs, a very low number of people who knew how to grab them. Between 1990 and 1994, male mortality rates rose 50%, and female rates by 25%. Heavy smoking, the highest rate of alcohol consumption in the world, and between 1992 and 1997, around 150,000 Russians were murdered. Gangster, lawless capitalism was the norm. Still, in 2010, the situation was not so good, though much better than it had been in the 90s. The new 2000 president, had put his iron fist on it. A majority of Russians loved him, mainly because he restored order and jobs. Jonathan the economist was very interested in these facts, related to the crook's discussions at the bar!

He cast a brief look at his tips: $1,025. Probably not bad for a Sunday. The Russians were very satisfied, Gerry too. More than $250 in tips only from this table on this evening. Indeed, they drank a lot, except Gerry, not totally being abstinent, but much more sober.

He went to the EXCEL file again.

No Chechen was not found on the list. But many Russians were in, more than a hundred. He found back one of them though, this time, saw a photo. Wow.

- Oleg Kulagin. Surname: Kee-Oleg. Russian émigré, billionaire. Former Gas-Prone Executive. Past life: unknown, KGB/FSB (Russian secret services) not excluded. His grandfather Boris was a member of the Okhrana, the former secret police of the last Tsar Nicolas II, until 1917. Officially: killed in 1917 by the Bolsheviks but in fact by Stalin's guys in the 1930s purges. Immensely rich, with several Swiss Banks accounts. Nothing about his father and mother. Last visit at the DD: October 15, 2007. Estimated revenues in 2008: 140 million. (Billy noted his own sources: NY Times, The Guardian UK, and some talks with him.) Wealth: 1.2 billion. VD.

So, it was the one Jonathan had seen on the list, looking at it at random, the first night he'd found Billy's wallet. And what did VD mean at the end? No idea. But he would find out. Other last letters noted by Billy, on other names, included ND, UK, SK. Humm. Will have to dig in out what's going on.

It had been close to three years since Billy had seen this Oleg at the DD. But he might have returned days after Billy was absent. By the way, how many hours was Billy clocking in? Five days a week, and the best ones. that is. So, chances were that, if Kulagin was in the DD, Billy would have seen him. Still, can't be entirely sure… and again, why was Billy collecting this murky information? Why? Why?

Jonathan searched the web.

He read up on the operations of the Russian and Chechen mafia, even on incognito, deleting every web trace and all cookies afterward. What he found was disturbing, frightening but confirmed what the guys said at the DD. "Protection" costs for the legal economy seemed to be at least 20% of the annual declared normal business income, taking on various forms, like providing women as sex slaves, handing out all kinds of goods, according to some articles, namely in the Guardian, and in fact differing depending on the country and sometimes per region. Smuggling was still almost everywhere in ex-USSR.

Mobs pay the police, the mayors and other municipal, provincial, and federal employees, truck drivers, local little warlords and various legal companies' officers, in apparently all ex-USSR countries.

There were many people involved at all steps, often paid by vodka packed in the rear of a truck, for example, at the border if problems were foreseen, and with US dollars or Euros, as well. Canadian dollars and British pounds would also do, at times.

The Guardian mentioned all kinds of guards, individuals in government and in private could be corrupted. Many who were all poorly paid, so they often made more than ten times their official salary with bribes in all ex-USSR countries. Except those who were protecting top government guys and top companies' executives, like those at Gas-Prone, who made a respectable salary and received (officially) no bribes.

Jonathan went to prepare for bed, brushing his teeth, exhausted from the day.

He fell asleep.

Dreaming strangely of Istanbul, pretty Turkish women; the Suez Canal; the Bab-El-Mandeb Strait; African wars for cocoa, oil and other basic products and a mix of Ukrainian vodka transported to New York, Chicago and South America aboard boats, trucks, and trains, and even of his old bike riding from Richford to his own apartment room in Manhattan, carrying unlawful smalls guns.

Few Days Off and Discussion with Mom

Monday, June 7th.

Jonathan was off. He was to work on Wednesdays to Sundays, inclusive.

He had called his mother in Vermont, on Sunday, late afternoon, since he was supposed to be back to Vermont on Monday.

As usual, he thought, *Mom will talk to me as if I were still a young boy...*

— Hi, Mom!
— Hello, dear son. So, when are you coming for a visit? Maybe for a bike ride now and then along Ayer's Hill Road?
— Well, yes, but, guess what. I have a new job in Manhattan.
— Wow! Great news, my favorite economist in the Big Apple. So, what is it?
— Well, not exactly an economist.
— How come, not exactly?
— Humm, Mom. I do bartending.

— A bartender! That's not a real job, you know. Is this just for a few days or weeks?
— Well, it's in a very respectable bar. I made good money this weekend and seriously am thinking about keeping it for a while.
— Jonathan Winkler, blood of by blood, flesh of my flesh, you'll not be a bartender for long, I can tell you. Why not find a real job, buy a country house around here, come the weekends?
— Mom, let me explain... I am no longer a young man, I know what I am doing!
— Sutton in Quebec was okay for Thursday nights and weekends in the ski lodges. It was nice and clean; you were at school and in love with Christine. And you did learn French on the pillow with her, but now, years later, no way you should. You'll find a real, new job as an economist, believe me. If not, if you're going to stay a bartender, all I can say is your father is going to have a heart attack.
— Mom, it's the DD. I don't know what to say. And Dad has a horse's heart. How is he?
— He's fine, mumbling a little as usual, but fine. What's the DD?
— A bar adjacent to the Waldorf-Astoria. There are a lot United Nations dignitaries who go there.
— Hmm. But a bar is a bar, you know. Strange girls, bad guys, cocaine, late nights. Nothing good.
— I know how to take care of myself, how to avoid trouble, Mom.
— And what about Christine?

— She's in L.A., working as a criminalist, you know that. It's all over between us, has been for a long time. Anyhow, I'm in my forties plus now!
— Jo, you know I know maybe not, well, not your heart. Distance and time may help it all to pass, but your mom says this: I saw that you loved her.
— Yes, loved, I admit. With a "d", at the end. But life goes on. Gimme two weeks, at least.
— Where are you staying during these weeks, hey? Manhattan isn't cheap. Little Italy? Chelsea? Soho? Greenwich Village? You're still straight, of course no drugs I guess?
— I told you the pay is good. So, I rented for a few weeks, Lower East Side, very nice place, and safe. And Mom, you know I only take a few drinks once in a while and have never touched the drugs. Won't start tomorrow!
— Safe. As Manhattan can be! Okay, but don't miss your opportunities to send out resumés, and visiting big, nice firms, good corporate citizens, of course.
— Of course, Mom, will do. I love you. I'll call back. Soon. Tell Dad. Or don't. As you wish.
— I'll tell him. You have your bike there, right? Though I imagine biking through the city is nothing short of reckless. So, another thing for me to worry about. You'll make me die earlier than I should.
— Don't worry so much. I'm fine. I'll be fine. A lot of bike lanes here in Manhattan, even taxis are used to bikes, everywhere here. And I take the bike through Central Park, then maybe, when I have time off, I'll ride to New Jersey, maybe to Pennsylvania.

— Be prudent. Cars have no pity. Nor trucks, buses, nor ambulances when you're not in them, nor motorcycles; even other bikes and pedestrian are dangerous. You're not on the Potato Hill Road here or in East Berkshire Village, you know.
— You've told me that a good one hundred times when I bike in the towns; you talk to me as if I was still in my twenties or even younger!
— One more time may not be enough. I want you back, in one piece. I know, my son, I should not talk like this, maybe, but, well, that's it, in your twenties or forties. My mother's heart will not change, I think! Will always love you as when you were a real kid. Think about a country house here, a stupid idea? We are getting old.
— Okay Mom, maybe. Love you too. Talk soon.

What Jonathan was thinking was that the danger may not be from his bike, but he said nothing, of course.

***

On Monday, June 7th Jonathan was up at 8 o'clock. He wasn't able to sleep anymore, even though he'd gone to bed around 4.

Want to do some biking, he thought. *Where?* The choices were many, though limited by the fact that he had to be at work at the bar on Wednesday, at 6 in the evening. He knew he'd have all the time in the world to walk in Manhattan and take the bike on some short runs, on work days, later.

So, why not take these two days for a little longer bike trip, out of NY?

He'd always wanted to visit as many of the state capitals as possible.

He'd already biked in Montpelier, of course, and to Concord, even Albany. Although no state could probably enjoy such a beautiful state house, an incredible piece of art as his home Vermont capital in his mind. He would like to compare, maybe all the way down to Washington or even farther. Using the car, the bicycle on top of it, riding around and putting it back on, at the end of the day.

What about other US states capitals? Albany, for the New York state? Too far for today, and already went there. New Jersey's capital, Trenton, was much closer, 50 miles away or so. Maybe too close, in fact, since he wanted to drive by car a bit too. Annapolis, in Maryland? Not bad, maybe, but remote.

Charleston, West Virginia, Columbus, Ohio, and Richmond, Virginia were all clearly interesting, but too far away for this time. The Adirondack and the Catskills mountains were tempting, too. But far a bit maybe, too, for the Adirondacks, and he already made a part of it years ago. But not the Catskills mountains, not yet.

Harrisburg, Pennsylvania's capital, appeared a good choice. But there'd be no way he could make it by bike and be home by Wednesday. A good 120 to 140 miles, more or less, if measured using a straight line.

He took the bus from Central Station to Harrisburg, hanging his bike with two others in front of the vehicle. He arrived about noon. It was great being in Pennsylvania again. But he'd never been here in Harrisburg. The last time he jumped in this state, it was in Philly, with Christine, and all her friends living there probably had moved.

But his thoughts were present, in attacking mode, non-stop. What was Billy? A spy? A mysterious CIA man? What else?

Pennsylvania state is almost a rectangle, with an area of 46,000 square miles, the 33rd largest US state. It had 51 miles of coastline along the Lake Erie, on its Northwest border, and 57 miles of shoreline along the Delaware river estuary, and, so, had a door on the Atlantic Ocean.

William Penn was the founder. On February 28, 1681, UK King Charles II granted a land charter to William Penn, in order to repay a debt of £16,000 owed to William's father, Admiral Penn. With a population of 12.6 million, it is the 26th state for the median income, so an average state for people revenues. 280 miles per 160 miles, approximately, with a rectangular form, although not perfectly. The day was sunny, extremely good weather for a bike trip.

He would try to visit the capitol as soon as he hopped out of the bus? As the pedals turned, he ducked in and out of some traffic, avoiding cars parked to the side for a mile before reaching a good bike trail, thoughts returned. When would the Turkish girls be back to the DD? Never?

He biked to City Hall, then along the Susquehanna River, crossed the Whitaker Center for Science and Arts, and passed the local attractions, like Market Square, where he stopped for a sandwich.

Harrisburg was all gussed up for the annual Pennsylvania Farm Show, possibly the largest agricultural exhibition of its kind in the US.

He remembered, too, that on March 28, 1979, the Three Mile Island nuclear plant, along the river, in Londonderry Township, just south of where he was, in Harrisburg, suffered a partial meltdown. And within days, 140,000 people had left the area. He remembered where he was when this tragical event happened.

At about 4 in the afternoon, he stopped at the Pennsylvania State Capitol, the main sightseeing attraction of his visit. He took in its Beaux-Arts style, built between 1902 and 1906, with some Renaissance themes.

He took in his hours' worth free visit, then returned to his leg engine. Gerry's plans were coming back to hit him.

And would he find a lady soon, someone pretty to ride within Manhattan? One who'd at least be interested in biking once in a while? Maybe a wife, for life, in NY?

He could only hope. Of course, he would. Be positive!

He'd taken bike tools along, just in case, and personal stuff in his bike-rack bags, not only the two on the side, but one on the back and one in front. The map was easily readable, on top of the little front bag. He'd pinned it there. Better than looking on his phone, too small. This map he'd bought before leaving, on Broadway, detailed all the roads between Harrisburg and a few cities around.

He went back zigzagging along backroads, some of them dirt roads, some asphalt, a sweet journey through picturesque villages and small towns, like Steelstown, Flintville, Reinholds, Shanesville and Greenlane. He avoided Reading. Too many cars and traffic.

He often stopped to watch the birds, listening to their trilling along the way. He spied a doe near the side of the road, one woodchuck, many squirrels, and, of course, many domestic animals when passing farmlands.

He saw a bobcat, probably a rare event, and heard several coyotes out in a group, used to these rural roads and woodlands. He remembered his own Ayers Hill Road, Skunk Hollow Road, Berry Road, northern Vermont, along the Canadian border.

So, he thought, what happened to Gerry, the young man he knew in Vermont? The one who didn't clean his room. Was he now an international smuggler? Seemed clear.

***

Jonathan spent Monday night in the small town of New Britain, in a pretty and comfortable bed and breakfast, $35 a night, close to the New Jersey border.

They had Internet, so he read a little about Russia, Smolensk, Ukraine, the White Sea, Peter the Great and his creation of St. Petersburg, the tsars and Lenin's 1917 Bolshevik revolution, the Kerensky provisional government, the kulaks (rich landowners in the early 1900s), the Russian and Chechen mobs.

But he was off work, and this was precious time to relax. So after about an hour or so, he elected to read several chapters of his short new book on relationships between employees and bosses, since he did have a new one.

But he realized this was a kind of work, after all, as well. So, he stopped.

He fell asleep, thinking about the youth of those Chechen mafia guys who would probably help the crook's smuggling. How would it compare to his own youth?

***

On the second day, June 8th, he decided to go to Trenton, New Jersey.

It was on his way back to NY, since he had ridden a little more south than he had expected. The New Jersey capitol was different, prone to New York City and Philadelphia urban behavior, much more influenced by this than was Harrisburg, Montpelier or Concord.

New Jersey is often thought of a 100%-urban state. In fact, it's nothing like that; some parts are still quite rural, and its motto, "Garden State," kind of hinted at this. Jonathan rode on some isolated roads but had to take many urban roads, more risky. And Mom getting older.

The second day of his trip was less beautiful than it had been along southern Pennsylvania, more disturbed by all the cars, but still nice, and he enjoyed it immensely.

The feel of the wheels, the pedals, everything speeding by, the time to think.

So, why had Billy taken down all that information?

Back in Manhattan, entering the island by bike during off-peak traffic hours, on Tuesday, early p.m., he decided to go to the DD, on his way back, for a coffee. He was dressed as a cyclist, wearing his cycling goggles, so the waitresses there didn't recognize him. No advertising on his clothes; Dad would probably not approve, lol!

The DD was very quiet in the afternoon, but two guys with a straight bowl-cut hairdo, FBI-looking, were at the bar, having a non-alcoholic beverage.

Jonathan took his black coffee and went home. He wanted no hassles today: best to stay clear of anyone talking about dirty plans.

At night, he watched CSI Miami. Horacio Kane was one of his favorites. Then bed, at 10. Biking some hilly 100 miles in two days hit him like a ton of bricks, though he was very pleased with his excellent shape.

Vermont dirt hills were still on his mind; he'd be back, definitely, again and again.

Where? All around. On many roads, he knew where the coming curve or the next intersection was, the next steep climb, and, quite often, the owner of the next farm or the next property.

One he could buy soon, as Mom suggested?

The Red Sea, Sudan, and Amanda

The DD was half empty at 6 in the evening, Wednesday night, June 9th, when Jonathan went to the jungle. The first two people to the bar after he started his shift came in laughing: two really funny guys.

— How much wood would a woodchuck chuck…? One said, sitting on the barstool.
— If… a woodchuck could chuck wood? Completed his friend.
— Jonathan shot out the answer.
— As much wood as a woodchuck would chuck, if a woodchuck could chuck wood.
— Great! You've got 50% more tips!
— Okay, guys, you look happy enough. Where are you from? Want a beer, wine, any shooters?
— Michigan. No jobs there in Flint, but it's a paradise here for two garbage removers, two entrepreneurs. We got a contract up in the Upper East Side for the next 2 years! Competitors are angry. We cut the prices. Got it.

The guy was quite excited.

— We'll bring our friends; they'll pinch in soon, and work hard with us, make some money, and leave the Big Apple with its garbage problems, after. We'll all go hunting near Sault-Ste-Marie, on Huron Lake and off the islands!
— I do like the Canadian border, too, Jonathan said.
— Where exactly?
— In Vermont, along the Quebec province ends, one hour and a half south of Montreal.
— So, *what does Quebec want*? Do you know?
— I do! Jo answered. They're asking for *grosso-modo*, for Quebec to separate from Canada, is it? Or more autonomy within Canada?
— You're about right, and some Vermonters may want to separate from the US of A too.
— Vermont, started the other guy, who now really seemed like an erudite sort of fellow, was an independent republic for fourteen years, between 1777 and 1791, you know.

Historians, too? Jo thought. *Strange garbage collectors.*

— I know. But let's have a B-52 shooter, and we'll see after.
— Okay, guys! Congratulations on your contract!

He was about to say he was born in Northern Vermont but refrained. After a few days only in this new place, conversations he overheard urged him to caution. Redhead

Gerry could be in at any time, sitting at the bar, or somewhere else, and he'd overhear, or talk with these buddies.

Trash guys were amazing, talking all the time, somehow seemed informed about the strangest intricacies of the US political system. Not stupid at all. Garbage removers: didn't mean they were only businessmen without knowledge.

At 7 on the dot, two tall Black men, apparently not from the US, given their dress, entered, with a White man. They asked for the church rood table. Jonathan had seen them pointing at it.

The waitress brought them to that specific table. Yep, exactly as he'd thought, that table would be what they'd request. But why were all these guys going to that one place? Jonathan walked over to their table, wiped it down, and spoke.

— Hello, gentlemen. I'll be your waiter tonight. What can I get for you?
— One Coors Light, the White man said.
— Black coffee, a big one, cream and sugar on the side, please. If you could bring it as hot as possible, I would appreciate, young man, the second guy said in a very good English accent.

Indeed, Jo still looked quite younger than his age.

— Orange juice, very cold, with a straw, please, said the third, apparently having some difficulties with Shakespeare's language.
— Fine. But I am no longer a young man! He throwed. Anything to eat? We don't serve complete meals

here, but many kinds of appetizers, tapas, and much more junk.
— We'll take nachos if you have them. Medium-spicy. With plenty of cheese.

Jonathan returned to the bar. The Michigan guys asked for a third beer.

— What time do you work tomorrow?
— Not tomorrow. Not even Thursday. Be back next Monday.
— Will we have you as our server whenever we're here?
— Why not? Jonathan said. I am the best at woodchucks!

Jonathan served the two men whom he'd figured out were somewhere from Africa, and the other White man. The table at the lower level was empty. But not for long.

Returning back to the bar, he suddenly came face to face with the pretty Turkish women group.

— Hi, Jonathan, said the one he'd been thinking of, the one with the devil's smile.
— Good evening, girls! Happy to see you're back. The DD is a very nice spot, I guess.
— Not especially, the one he'd been thinking about said.

And, getting up onto her toes, as much as she could from her 5'3" stature, she said softly in his ear:

— But some bartenders are.
— Okay, he smiled, a little shy. I'll get back to you. Have to serve the table up there first, then the guys at the bar; and after that, all of you!

As this, the little woman sat down. Her friends quickly asked what she had whispered into his ear.

— I... if we could have the same table as last time.
— Sure, sure, they said, amazed, not convinced.

Jo returned to them, minutes later. The table on the upper level was deep in conversation, and he had to curb himself from stretching his neck to hear what the guys were saying, as he responded to the ladies.

Up above, one of the men was talking very softly. Jonathan caught some words, important ones, it seemed, scattered here and there.

— What can I get you, girls?
— Four cold beers. All Alexander Keiths, please. Two blondes and two ambers.
— You're all from Turkey, aren't you? Heard so last time, I think.

He was washing the table; it wasn't clean enough, not according to his standards.

— Of course not! Said the one who'd just whispered in his ear. But I am. My name's Amanda. And this is Samantha, from Utah; Clara, born in Frankfurt, lived

fifteen years in Sweden and Anastasia, whose parents are from the Ukraine, but she's lived in Turkey for many years, and she is now quite Turkish. We're the A's group. I mean, all of our names end in A!
— Like the Swedish musical group ABBA, Clara said.
— And not Frankfurt, Kentucky, but Frankfurt in Germany, she added.
— Okay. Taking note. How old are you, may I ask?
— No, you can't! Clara said, laughing.
— Okay. I know I shouldn't have. Anyway, I'm far too old for you... but may refer you to my friends, lol.

Light conversations like this always eased things up a bit, regardless of Jonathan's real intent this time, to linger just a little bit longer, so he could catch the snippets from above, and chat with the girls.

— You never know! Many younger women like mature men; it's well known! We're all in our late 20s. Except Amanda. A little older. 36. But she does not tell; she looks 26, or so.
— Great! I'll go get the beers. Sorry about asking stupid questions.
— In my short lifespan, I've heard many more stupid things, Amanda said, mischievously.

He went back at the bar, Amanda passed by and left him a phone number, on a piece of paper, with a shy smile.

From the table above, the words had been really striking. Making his way back to the bar for the Keiths, he analyzed what he'd caught: St. Petersburg, Riga, boats, cars, Gdansk, Gibraltar, Cape Town, guns, the Sudan, oil, pipelines, United Nations, Red Sea, Suez Canal, and... Operation Dark Snakes.

Wow. Things were getting really serious, and more and more people involved, it seemed.

St. Petersburg, Russia! The tsar's capital for centuries, established in 1703 by Peter the Great, to open the sea for Russia because the Black Sea was controlled by the powerful Ottoman Empire. Jo should have included it his list of harbors. Clearly. The arms would travel only in Russia, from Smolensk to St. Petersburg. Easier. Probably cheaper.

But much longer than to Odessa or to other ports? And how would they reach a country in Africa and Prince Marty, then? Much more complicated, uneasy, costly.

— Everything's okay for you now? He asked the garbage guys at the bar.

They were getting a little drunk, but there was some sobriety left somewhere.

— Yes, enough alcohol, one told Jonathan. We have to go now. We don't usually spend our wages before cashing them, and, normally, we don't drink much.
— Thanks team! Hope to see you again soon.
— Sure, man! But maybe for a few beers less, next time.
— No problem. Take care.

The two exited onto the street. Seconds later, several gun shots were heard, not far away, maybe 200 feet. A few clients did look at the window; one of them even opened the door, carefully, a few minutes after. Two men had been shot in the head, said someone to Jonathan. Close to the bar.

Jonathan feared the worst. *The Flint sympathetic guys,* he thought, horrified. Competitors shot?

But he had to wait until the tomorrow's newspapers, probably, to know more. Or on the web in the next hours.

He then found a small paper note on the ground, under the upper table, at about ten to 1 in the morning, and put it into his pocket. He closed up at 2 a.m. and went home.

Central Park

Jonathan got back to the apartment, the morning night of Thursday, June 10th.

What an evening!

Not so great in terms of tips, $500, but not at all bad for a Wednesday, and so many things had happened. Guns. Shootings; had those garbage men possibly been killed for a mere 2 years contract in Manhattan? The Chechens. St. Petersburg. Gibraltar. Operation Dark Snakes.

His blood went ice-cold thinking of all of this. And the phone number from Amanda. Unexpected, but how welcome. She had that kind of smile, and eyes, cheeks, he could forget his fears for a moment, however brief.

He went over Billy's list again.

One of the Black men he'd seen at the bar the other night was there, his photo, not much more. From Sudan, or Ethiopia, or Somalia, Billy had written. No name. Jonathan hoped the young women, were not on the list! No! No! Say it ain't so.

He sorted through the list, going first by country, then by state, really going through the names and descriptions, carefully. Nothing on these young women. Thanks God.

Now for the piece of paper. He took it out carefully, unfolded it. Written on a blue back, with red ink. What if the guy finds he lost it, figures out he'd lost it at the bar? Risky. Jonathan scanned it, using his computer, and refolded it exactly as it was. He would put it into the lost items at the bar tomorrow, along with a few other faked notes he would write. If the guy came back, and asked, a waitress, not him, in charge, would return it after a short description. No risk then?

It looked strange, very strange. There was only one sentence, a question, obviously, as it ended with question mark; and there were wide spaces between the four words.

AZQX BAFTA SI WKYLF?

No known language. Surely, it was code. He would look at it later. Time to move on to more fun things.

He had Amanda's cell phone number. She said in the conversation at the table she was a teacher, and wonders of wonders, also a cyclist! And so attractive to him. She seemed definitely intelligent, and he was sure she liked first of she saw in him. Let's not forget, her words whispered into his ears! A friend? maybe more? Dreaming a bit was free.

He would call her tomorrow. And propose a bike ride? Yep. Maybe, by some miracle, she was off from work on Mondays, or Tuesdays. Well, he thought, anyway, he had her number. Wasn't that some sort of, well, miracle?

Okay, don't dream too hard, man. But call. She must be free one of those days, certainly somewhere on weekends. Just contact her and see.

***

June 10, Thursday morning, 9:50 a.m.

Jonathan called Amanda. Just before 10, he thought. If she's at home, great, and there was no real chance he'd wake her up. If she were out, on the job, well, she'll no doubt get the message. So, he was half prepared, half not. The phone rang.

— Hello?
— Hello, Amanda. It's Jonathan.
— Jonathan… who?
— Humm, he murmured, embarrassed. From the DD bar. You remember?
— Um, no, no. I was probably drunk, you know.
— I'm sure you were not. I'm the bartender at the DD bar… you left me your phone number… humm… I just wanted to…

She cut him off, with a sunrise voice.

— I'm joking. I certainly remember you. It's funny you're calling now. What time did you close, if I may ask?
— 2 a.m. And you? At work this morning?
— No, a kind of holiday but paid. I'm using the time to review notes and new teaching ideas. What about your own day? How's that going?
— I'll be in at work at 6 tonight. Maybe I'll go biking around this morning, maybe this afternoon, if the

sky clears, he tried, as an introduction for a tour he heavily hoped she'd say yes to.

He noticed his heart rate was quite high, just thinking about a bike ride with her! C'mon, what's that?

— If the sky clears? If I were waiting for a blue sky, I wouldn't be out cycling that often.
— What kind of riding do you do?
— I have two bikes, one for asphalt: faster, with smaller tires. And a kind of mountain bike I use on the city streets and paved lanes too, but much more on the dirt roads and tough hills you can't find in Manhattan. And you?

Jonathan felt as though he'd had a heart attack. A woman like her, biking along unpaved, dirt roads, she said. Lost somewhere with him, behind a hill, talking about Turkish history and Mustapha Kemal. Was it real?

— Hello, are you still there? Her voice was soft, cheerful.
— Ah... yes! Maybe we had a moment's wrong connection.
— What a lie! It was a fine connection.
— What a coincidence, he said then. I use a mountain bike, too, and dirt roads are my favorite. And hills, love them, believe it or not.
— No, I don't believe it, she said, laughing. What a coincidence, indeed. You may have to prove it, laughing again. Cyclists are much more numerous

on paved tracks. They all say they are good at hills, but in fact, probably not. I'm using my road bike less and less, and more and more my mountain bike for safer rides, for little holes on the road, more conscious of traffic dangers now, maybe.

He jumped, as the occasion she had just presented.

— So, when would you like to take a look?
— Take a look at what?
— My mountain biking techniques, let's say.
— What about now?

Second heart attack. Worse than the first. But he survived.

— Are... are y-y-you in Manhattan right now, Amanda? He stammered.
— Yes. I'm not far from the DD, in Midtown.
— So, could I suggest we meet at the southeast corner of Central Park, on 59th, south of the MET? How long do you think you need?
— Give me 40 minutes, tops. Can you beat this, nimble bartender?
— Don't think so, Ma'am. I'm in Midtown, too. But, let's say, 50, 60 minutes max?
— Okay, so I'll see you then?
— Yep. See you there.

Jonathan could hardly believe it. In all actuality, he'd only need 15 minutes to get pedal-to-the-medal, to Central

Park. But had to prepare, dress fine, bring a water bottle, maybe two apples, some nuts, bananas.

Manhattan was full of bike lanes. And life full of surprises. The sky was clearing, the sun shining over one of the world's most glorious parks, with hours of views they could sightsee while biking along. Was life smiling to him?

At 10:30, when he arrived, Amanda was there on a nice bike, blue and white, with a light, metal-grey wheels protector. And with a bell, speedometer, cell phone stand, and some other equipment. She certainly rode often. She hadn't been lying, at least on this.

At night, in the DD, she was cute, attractive. At day, under the sun, wearing yellow cycling clothes and black pants, and a gray helmet, she appeared even better looking, if that was even possible. *Maybe not an athlete,* he thought, *not too far though. 5'2, maybe 5'3.*

And that wonderful smile, again.

— Hi, sir!
— Hello, Amanda. Jonathan Winkler.
— So, the barmen have family names? Glad to learn of it. Amanda Ciller here.
— Ciller, as in Tansu Ciller, the past president of Turkey, a woman?
— Yes, you're absolutely right. But I guess you don't know much more than that about Turkey, in what year was she elected?
— Humm, '92, I think.
— You're almost right about that too! In fact, it was '93.

So, this guy read about Turkey yesterday, minutes ago, or he's really informed, or reads much, or both, Amanda thought.

— Where would you like to make it? Right here? Central Park?
— Sure. The easiest, closest, and not too busy now. If you agree.
— Okay then. Let's go.

They took a path snaking toward the MET. They biked slowly, side by side, keeping up a conversation, as there was a very low bike traffic, and few pedestrians.

— What kind of gold machine is it? Jo asked, once in the park. Quite different. Never seen that model or similar.
— It's a Schwinn from Vietnam. Not really a mountain bike. In fact, I own a small collection, including this and the other mountain bike I told you about. This one only has three speeds. Clearly enough for Manhattan. Flatland.

Amanda laughed.

— Yeah, he said. I can't prove anything today, no hills, nor dirt roads here.
— But I can see those calves!

Jonathan blushed.

— Ah, he smiled.
— Hillers have good ones, normally, she said.
— Thanks!
— Speaking of dirt, unless you did put some on your bike minutes ago, there's some proof there. Amanda lifted her chin toward his back tire. Where'd you go recently?
— Pennsylvania, on Monday and Tuesday. On some dirt roads. But you may notice two dirt colors clearly different, the other one comes from Northern Vermont and Canada. I was born there. I should wash it better.
— You were born in Canada, in the Quebec province?
— No. In Vermont. Two miles south of the border. We both still have plenty of dirt roads there, fantastic hills to climb and go down, magnificent views, on both sides of the border. One site, indeed, on Claybank road in Frelighsburg, Quebec, give a fantastic view on our Vermont hills. The Canada and US border sign is on a little white marker, on the top of the hill, about 15 feet away from the dirt road. And both countries, I think, offer a similar foreign policy.
— Would be glad to climb this hill, maybe one day. A good foreign policy, according to you?
— We-ell, it's about the same, up and down, I'd say, but overall I judge it good.

It was June, and there were already a lot of flowers, with their own charming smells. Squirrels and singing birds were busy all around, though some cars, of course.

— Where do you find hilly dirt bike roads? Jo asked.
— Everywhere I can. Not possible here. But in Tennessee, actually. A few times went to Canada, too, in the Coaticook region, south of Sherbrooke, a city in Quebec. Do you know this small town, Coaticook?

They turned right, then left, then right but did not really care where they were going. As long as they stayed in Central Park, discussed, and were together, everything was perfect.

— No. Or... not sure, Jo said. Going northeast from Richford, I think.
— Where's Richford?
— Sorry, it's the small town where I was born. Straight north from Montpelier, our Vermont capital, and maybe a little east. I used to ride just outside the Richford village, on Ayer's Hill road, where I trained these legs! Along the Canada border.
— Sure, I know Montpelier. I've been there with friends. But I do not know Richford.
— I would say Coaticook is northeast from Richford, in Canada, the province of Quebec, close to the border, would say 10–15 miles. Not far from the New Hampshire border actually.
— Hmm, yes for roads, but I don't know about bars in Coaticook! By the way, I'm not a real bartender.

— What do you mean? You do your work so well in a busy, international, diplomat's bar. And I saw you looking at all the other women around.

Her voice rose, jokingly.

— Nah, really, I'm humoring you, but you do bartend very well, especially for someone who's so inexperienced, as you claim you are.
— I meant I could have done other things, more useful to society. Teach, for example.
— Teaching? I show English as a second language, to students from other countries. On my own and in the public schools.
— Teenagers. Been doing it, on and off, for two years. Don't worry. I'm not changing society and all that, not like they say. So, bartending? And you're not new to bartending, huh? So, tell me about how a nice-looking guy, who knows who the prime minister of Turkey is and who they were, who seems to know a lot about foreign politics, is or becomes a bartender? Temporary? Permanent? Indulge my curiosity.

Jo could feel his face growing red.

— Well, really, it's luck of the draw. Or bad luck of the draw. Don't know. I'm an economist. Or "econo-missed." I haven't in this field for more than three years! I've just finished a Masters in Burlington, back to school after my company cut a

lot of "unnecessary jobs." International Economics, then, last week, all that changed when I accepted a full-time job at the DD. We'll see. I've been there five days. Only.
— Five days, it's not like five years working at a corporation, huh? But how did you get in this strange job, for an educated economist? I don't get it!

He smiled. So, she was really listening to all details. They were passing along Turtle Pond, then close to the Obelisk. Striking colors, still. Lovers walking, hand in hand. Or loners, taking in some fresh air. A male sparkling red cardinal flitted along the path, a few meters away, said a few words of his own.

Jo explained what had happened with Billy, then all the rest. But, of course, nothing about the list, the table on the upper and lower levels, the acoustics of the DD, Gerry and the like.

— What a strange story! Amanda threw out into the wind. So, are you going to stick there, at the DD?
— With the great wages and a pretty woman from Turkey coming around, mind you in the five days I've been there, only a fool would leave!

He'd said this rather awkwardly and, too late, gulped down any other words that would sound so silly.

She laughed. Even from the seat of his bike, with the breeze in their faces, passing slower cyclists every now and then, he could see that she'd become a little shy, too. But, of course, she hadn't thought about the good salary.

— So, yeah, mine in teaching's not so great. They don't pay so much for teachers here, I could say, not at all, but we get something: a little here, a little there. I may have problems soon keeping my small apartment. I could try selling some of my bikes from my collection.

She laughed again.

— I've got a few; unbelievable, but I've found space for them in my small flat and in storage. Plus, they need a few repairs, maintenance, you know.
— Oh, don't. Don't sell them. Not now. I'd really like to have a look at them, someday, maybe. I repaired mine and others when I was in Vermont, and still do.

They were back at the Metropolitan Museum, just behind it, along the paved path. The sun was still shining between some clouds, with the high-rises as a background.

— My bike collection is in Tennessee.
— Why there?
— My uncle has a farm, close to Chattanooga. He stores them in his barn. A good place to keep them in top shape. I go there several times a year, work on some, bring one or two back, keep them on my balcony, or leave them at my uncle Jim's for the

winter. Of course, I don't bring the expensive ones here. Too likely to get stolen. But I should, maybe, and sell them in the Big Apple? Could make a lot of money, I guess.
— How much can a nice bike like yours cost, if I can be so bold as to ask?
— Well, let's see. You'll never believe this, but I own an old vegetable from World War I, this bike built in 1915.
— Really?
— Yeah, no kidding, and used by Russian soldiers, worth at least $12,000, probably if I sold it here. The nephew of the nephew of the last tsar, or his son, or so my uncle tells me. We are not totally sure about it.

Short silence from Jonathan. Just, amazing, maybe, to repair a bike from the last Russian dynasty.

— So, it's 12:35, Jonathan said. And we've done, well, 15 miles, or so. I'm not tired, but are you hungry?
— Oh, you guys, always hungry. Not me, not yet! I suggest we continue for another hour when the lunch rush is over. We could get something at a small restaurant, grab a sandwich. So, if we do long enough, I could verify your lies about your long running and biking abilities. I don't want to bring someone somewhere not able to sweat more than two mini hours a day in hills like those in Tennessee.

She spoke the last sentence looking quickly at the ground, even as she was riding. Very shy.

— Done deal! Jonathan said, simply.

Sometimes, as she was talking, he was thinking about Billy and the chain of events, making sure not to show it, though. Trying to get rid of it!

They spotted a new, small, orange and green café inside an old Victorian style house, close to the New York Historical Society, on 75th. They were now sitting, face to face, in a little corner of this pretty café, in a quiet street, in the heart of Manhattan.

— Two black coffees, sir, Amanda asked the waiter. And could you bring us the menus, please?
— Okay, miss! I hope it won't bother you too much if I'll be with you in a few minutes, suggested the barista, an older mom who immediately saw the probable match, looking at the smiles and at this young couple's behavior.

Still thinking, while talking... about the arms, Billy and the rest, Jonathan decided to try to avoid the subject with Amanda. Of course. At least for now, for sure.

— I will try the salmon salad. Not much more, Amanda said.
— A turkey sandwich, please! Requested Jonathan.
— Turkey is a nice country, but, sadly, they let too much smuggling go through the Black Sea, and

corruption is still too important, though the situation clearly and steadily improving, Amanda said.

Less romantic, maybe, but the door was open, and, in front of her deep-set eyes, he did not much know what to say. Aside from Christine, he'd had few or no real fulfilling relationships with women. And he was no expert at the cruising bar, not at all.

As for the discussion leaning toward Turkey as subject or the Black Sea or the Bosporus Strait or her friend Anastasia from the Ukraine, or... could it happen? He guessed it could go on... smuggling. But, really, what he was wondering was how to make this more chat romantic. He dove a bit.

— You were born there in Turkey? Why did you mention smuggling is so disturbing?
— Yes, in Istanbul, 1974. We lived several years, then, in Erzurum, close to the Kurdistan region, not too far from the Iran, Armenia and Georgian borders.
— Yes, Georgia adjacent to Azerbaijan, on the Caspian Sea?
— Not exactly. Georgia lies on the Black Sea, not the Caspian, but Azerbaijan does! Then we left Turkey, when I was still young. My father was a government employee, working as an administrator in a hospital. He became discouraged with the Kurdish situation and found a nice job in a small local hospital near Knoxville, Tennessee. My uncle was already there, so we joined him. They're among the few immigrants in Tennessee but did receive a nice

welcome by several neighbors. They spoke a correct English, and it helped. I studied in Atlanta. The Russian mob now is in many countries and many cities, including Atlanta, and Istanbul. My uncle says the smuggling in increasing on the Black Sea, and a few respectable newspapers such as the Kiev Post say so too, but prudently.

— What materials? Drugs?

— Anything. Russia has relatively limited access to the Black Sea, a rather short, harsh shore, one potential reason why they want to develop the Sochi region more, along the Black Sea, where the Winter Olympics will be held in 2014. Or take back Crimea. But today, the Ukraine has a very long shore on the Black Sea, and you can make pass all kinds of goods there, from Russia and Central Asian ex-USSR republics, to who knows where. Anastasia's friends are still in the Ukraine; they know a lot but don't talk, as everybody do. A bit dangerous.

— Hmm. And what about smuggling goods to the North, to St. Petersburg or Latvia or even Poland, for example. Do you know about this?

— Possible, yes, but more risky. And it changes all the time. But If I would be doing something underground, sending something through the black market, I would choose the Black Sea, by the Dnieper, road, train, or whatever. And I would have to pay the protection! But don't we get to talk about more positive, sunny subjects, gentleman?

— Yeah, sure.

— But thanks for your interest for my home country, I appreciate.

They talked until 3 at the café, eyes staring into eyes. A host of themes: their mothers, their fathers, Vermont, a little more on Turkey, Tennessee, Obama, Bush, biking, a bit of romance, flowers, chocolate... and, finally, she said the word: they needed to go.

— Are you up for a little more biking? Fresh legs? Anyway, we have to get back. And you work at 6, right?
— Yep. Okay, let's go.

At 4:30, they ended the tour, parting on the same southeast Central Park corner, with a promise of a rendezvous in the following days.

Brown Envelopes

Thursday night went smoothly for Jonathan, but it was busy, noisy, happy atmosphere.

No bad guys, no potential trouble.

He listened as usual to the clients' jokes. This was one of the best parts of the job, for him.

> — Two Mooseheads, please. Do you know the two psychologists' joke?
> — No.
> — Two old friends, both psychs, meet up again after a few years.
> — Where, at a bar?
> — Yeah, could be at the bar. So, they look carefully into each other's eyes for a good 30 seconds. Then one says, "I see you're fine. What about me?"
> — Yeah, this one is brainy!

Despite overhearing the jokes, listening closely to some, he was thinking about the plan. Many thousands of people would probably die because of the arms warehoused in Smolensk, if they reached their final destination, or, rather, their many final destinations. If.

How to ensure they wouldn't? How to make sure the crooks were caught? Was it even in his capacity to do anything to have plans crushed? He thought of the prof in his management course. "How, who, when, why... with what money?"

Contemplating ways to block the plan became a kind of a management project, and Jonathan was going to be the project manager. The leader. An anonymous one, but a leader, nonetheless. And the project had to be a success. He would give himself the grade he would merit.

The "Why" was obvious. As for the "When"? As soon as possible; he should start as soon as possible. But the "Who" and the "How," well, he had to think.

Really, if he thought about it, "How" was dependent on "Who." So, who would go to the bat on this project? For the moment, of course, he was alone. Totally.

Two guys came in, one wearing a T-Shirt, with "Beer is now cheaper than gas. So, drink. Don't drive," darkly written on it.

— Two Perriers, please, said the "Beer now cheaper" guy. Jonathan smiled.
— But you're not going to order any alcohol? Your shirt is a liar, then.
— No, I don't drink any alcohol. This old rag is a good joke, I use it to convince people to think about it and stay under the legal level.
— Great! So, two Perriers, say, with lemon on the side?
— Yep.

Jonathan was mulling over a few ideas.

What about the local police? They probably wouldn't take it at all seriously, and it was above their reach and responsibility, anyhow.

What if he contacted an investigative journalist? Without risk to himself, of course. Okay. Good idea. But having read a book, a kind of *"What Google and Other IT Companies Know About You,"* he was concerned about using email. He'd read that cookies and other traces were always left when you visit websites, and these could identify your computer, etc., etc. Even apparently anonymous emails like Hotmail and Gmail were not really anonymous. So, if not by email, how?

But was he exaggerating these risks? Maybe.

Then, what about a good, old-fashioned phone call?

Or the even better antique method: a brown envelope?

Not something stupid. He'd send the info by regular US mail, maybe? To a well-known, solid, investigative journalist. But how to verify he would take it seriously and would run a follow-up?

Two buddies sat at the bar. Engineers from South Carolina, apparently.

— Two gins and tonic, please.
— Do you know the difference between "For free" and "For nothing"? asked the first, facing his buddy.
— Would say no.
— I went to school for free because of a private donor. You went for nothing.
— Ha! Ha! I like that one.

Yes, that's it. He'd ask a famous New York Times writer. Jim Barker would be a good choice. And for a proof Barker was taking his information about the smuggling seriously, Jonathan would request that the Times journalist use particular words in a sentence in one of his next one or two articles to come. Easy enough, and nobody nefarious, not in a million years, would be able to figure things out. Which first keywords? What about this: "Uncertain Seas"? He would read every paper from Barker then. Easy-peasy; no risk, none at all.

Now the next point was what detail or details should be included, to make sure Barker was taking the whole thing and act? And did Jonathan even have enough info yet?

An older man from Ohio, retired from the mining industry, was sitting at the bar.

— A Budweiser please.
— One Bud coming up!

A couple days ago, at the church rood table, one of the guys had talked about the way to keep arms and munitions in working order after more than twenty years, particularly with respect to the humidity level. Too high a level would, obviously, cause the powder to rot, also creating rust inside and other problems. But he also said that a level of humidity that was too low, particularly for Kalashnikov bullets manufactured between 1978 and 1990, would alter the chemical composition and render the whole gun dangerous and potentially explosive, certainly much less effective if it worked at all. Jo had searched the web then.

This was all difficult detailed information to find, for the layman, that is. But it could be verified by an investigative team, and if convincing, well, Jo had a good chance to see Barker take it and write the key words "Uncertain Seas" in one of his next columns, he thought.

— Here is your tip, man! Don't worry, be happy! You know that song? See you! Said one of Jonathan's now regular clients.
— Sure I do, thanks, and take care.

But what if the whole thing doesn't work? Would he need a Plan B, one he'd developed later?

Now for this: what other details should he include in this brown envelope?

Jonathan was deep in thought. The city of Smolensk, the Black Sea, the White Sea, Riga... in fact, his words should be good enough to put and investigative team on the track, then send more envelopes as more mobsters and information could come to light in the DD.

Barker could put Interpol interested on it, no? Sure, it was all possible. He really wanted Prince Marty and the crooks' plans to be foiled.

Should he add in his info to Barker something about Armando and Company?

It could be a key item. Yep, try it.

When he'd been looking for information a couple of days ago, Jo had found only one or two short sentences about Armando from his own search, written in the UK Guardian newspaper. The piece had been written by the editorial team: "... some murky companies, such as, let's call them

Harmendoo and Co., could sell almost any goods, anywhere, as soon as they are expensive and unlawful."

They looked prudent in not even mentioning Armando itself, instead using the word "Harmendoo" as a cover. Maybe Barker would call the Guardian editorial team.

Yes, it could work.

Add some details on the guys who came at the DD, and on Billy's list? This should be good for a NY Times brain writer as Barker, no? Possibly.

Well, too many thoughts. Contact Barker first, with limited, clear, credible info; then, see. Okay then.

— Hello! Said a young lady. A Pinot noir, please.
— Be right with you!

Back at the apartment, he checked his tips, as usual. $800! Plus, two free tickets to the NY Rangers hockey game next Thursday. And two tickets to the MET from a couple unable to go. These were the best of the best. He smiled. He'd invite Amanda to the MET.

He went back to his own plan.

***

He prepared his first brown-envelope letter to Barker.

Two billion dollars' worth of arms from the ex-USSR at stake: hundreds of thousands of people could die.

Hello, Mr. Barker. I often read your column in the Times. I read many of your analyses and investigations, including the last one that helped send the governor of Nebraska to jail, and another one that forced the senator of Missouri to resign.

I have no idea how many letters like this you receive every day or every week. This one is serious, very serious. It involves murky connections here and abroad. A large amount is involved; I've heard about $2 billion in arms to be sent in Africa, or a part of it. So, possibly thousands of innocent people will be killed, maimed, or displaced, becoming refugees, depending on where and how the arms would be used. I know for sure they are intended to be sold on the black market to a powerful murky prince, somewhere in Africa, very soon.

Yes, I know. This may all look like a joke, the ramblings of an insane man. But I have serious reasons to believe all of this, reasons that I will elaborate right here.

He went on.

Where I work, in a Manhattan bar, I overheard some guys (when they had no idea I could hear them, of course; there is a strange acoustics effects in that bar at a few key places) talking about ways to keep arms and munitions in working order after their being out of commission for twenty years, heard them ruminating about the humidity level and its effect on the arms.

They spoke about too high a level of humidity causing rust and leading to other problems. They were also saying that too low a level of humidity, dryness, particularly for Kalashnikov bullets manufactured between '78 and '90 or so, meant the chemical composition of powder and metal was changing, rendering them dangerous and possibly explosive, as well as much less effective if they worked.

All this info on Kalashnikov bullets is difficult to find for the layman. But, if possible, it should be verified by an investigative team such as yours. The thing is, we may only have a mere days, maybe a few weeks, to stop a deadly attack somewhere in Africa.

An important part of these arms is apparently located in Smolensk, Russia, in a secret, perhaps underground warehouse.

He followed with this…

A Chechen mob would probably be in charge of paying the warehouse guards to stand around and just look the other way, as the warehouse were emptied, and deliver the stuff then, or kill them. We don't know many other details of the operation, but we know that a wealthy African prince is purchasing the stuff, setting up the travel plans through the Black Sea toward Africa, or along the White, Baltic or other sea passage. In at least one African country, this would destroy. We don't yet know the countries. Armando Co. is involved, but we don't know how, not yet.

We'll probably be getting information every day or so and will send you more, if you agree to give us a sign in one of your next two papers, this week. You would only have to use the following two words together anywhere in your column: "Uncertain Seas." This will signal to us that you have taken this information seriously.

Once this happens, you will then receive other brown envelopes, with more info as we get it. We suspect the operation to start in the next two weeks. This is urgent.

Thank you.—Jo the pigeon

***

On Friday morning, June 11th, Jonathan dressed like a much younger man.

Sunglasses, a baseball cap, reversed; he'd let his beard grow a bit longer.

He took his bike, left his cellphone at home and, around 10 in the morning, rode off to the New York Times' headquarters.

There were security checks at the entrance. Certainly cameras. Humm. He could be identified later on.

Long story short, he didn't go in, chose instead to ask and pay somebody on the street to leave the envelope at the front desk. The first possible guy was clearly a tourist to New York.

— Hi, sir, would you mind my asking, where are you from?

No answer. The man continued to walk.

— Hi, ladies. How are you?

No answer. But this city was busy. Surely, there would be someone here, some tourist who'd be interested. There were so many events leading them to the city.

On his fifth trial, Jo thought he'd change the approach. Husband and wife, no doubt in their 60s, walking slowly, watching everything around them.

— Hello, lady and gentleman. Would you like to make 20 dollars right now?
— Maybe. What's the catch? What's the scam?

— Nothing. No trick. Just leave this letter in the next office at the New York Times reception. Information about the local contracts from the NY mayor. I really don't want to go in myself. I know too much, there are cameras, lol. May I ask where you're from?
— Tallahassee, Florida. We're now retired; I was a part-time teacher, and my husband worked for the city for 30 years, responsible for the city's parks. We have, say, fishy, local contractors, too. The man laughed.
— New York's not any better than our Tallahassee, he said too.
— We will do it for $30, she risked. I manage finances.
— Okay, here is the first half, 15 boxes. I'll wait here with your husband, if that's alright with you. It's just there, next door. Jonathan pointed out the entrance.
— There's a security guard who'll take it. They certainly often receive that kind of information, anonymous, at the Times.

The woman sneaked in, delivered. Jonathan had prepared the little package in the following way: a brown envelope, unidentified, which enclosed another envelope, with Jim Barker's name on it, and 'CONFIDENTIAL' in big letters. So, she could not see Barker's name, and nothing more. He was able to watch every one of her moves.

She returned. Jonathan gave her the second $15, simply, smiling.

— Have a nice day!

He went to get his bike. His cellphone rang. Amanda.

— Hello, Jonathan! How are you?
— Fine, and you?
— Pretty good, thanks. I'm having a hot chocolate, reading the papers.
— Any interesting news I should be aware of? He asked.
— Yes. Locally, municipal taxes will increase in Manhattan, apparently due to a big hole in the municipal budget. Totally unexpected, said the mayor.
— Usual stuff. Where are you reading this? Who's the journalist?
— Barker, NY Times, and I read a few other columns.
— Yes, I know him, read him sometimes.
— So, Jo, are you busy today?
   Humm, that's nice: "Jo," he thought.
— At 6 this evening, I become a bartender in a shabby bar. Full of rats. You know, not animals, but men.
— Yes, I know, and doubtful women too. I am one of them. She laughed.
— But before 6, well not really busy. Humm... why do you ask? He was still a bit shy with her.
— I'm off between now and 1 tomorrow afternoon.
— Have you been to the MET? Quite sure you have, but just wondering.
— Not yet. Mea culpa. Too many things to do in the Apple.

— Are you ready to go?
— Kind of. Now, you mean?
— Why not? Don't we have 5 hours to kill.
— Sure, it'd be very nice. See you there at 11? And we each pay for ourselves, Dutch style?
— Yes, humm, no. Amanda, in fact, well, I'm not a very good liar. I came into free tickets at the bar last night and wanted to invite you.
— Well, it's the intention that counts! I don't care. And I'm excited!
— See you at 11?
— Yep! Working. See you.

They met at the museum and went walking through the galleries, exchanging comments and knowledge on the Picasso and Renoir expositions, taking a rest along the gallery benches to extol on the Black Sea, on Istanbul, to flirt, to discuss the Canadian and Mexican borders, flowers, politics, cooking, to engage in more flirting, to talk about Robert Kennedy and Rose Kennedy, fine cheese, poverty in Africa, Mustapha Kemal new Turkish alphabet in the 1920s, Istanbul history, to flirt some more, to sometimes gaze into each other's eyes, sometimes shyly looking away at the wood floors.

Clearly, they were immensely enjoying each other's presence, and the conversation.

She reached over and took his hand.

— You can call me Mandy.
— And as you have already, you can call me Jo.
— I already had?

- Yes, you did.
- Sorry if it was, say, inappropriate.
- Not at all. He smiled.

They made their way back to their bikes. She didn't have the Schwinn she'd used the other day, but, locked up, was a very different one, red and yellow and lower to the ground, with three speeds. It looked a bit like it was a 1930s vintage to Jo (as he now thought of himself; he liked that nickname and thought about the various people in his past who'd called him that, but it had never really stuck, until now perhaps).

- Oh! So, what's this beautiful bike? There's no way for me to tell what brand or mark. So, what is it?
- Try to find out, Mr. Bartender, and call me back! She said playfully, her smile totally disarming and inviting.

Jonathan took a photo of the bike, intending to have fun on the net discovering its make and model, even its history and price, and where to find parts.

***

At 5, he was back at his apartment, changing clothes.

He took five minutes to read Barker's column in the Times: something on NY municipal taxes—it was a short paper, a killer.

The mayor should have known, Barker had written.

There was a hole of 8 billion dollars out of a total annual budget of 80 billion for all of New York City, or 10%! Unacceptable, huge mistake, or worse, he declared.

And at the end, in the last sentence, Barker wrote, "The mayor knows honest taxpayers are navigating on **uncertain seas**, but he should not forget they have an idea about how to drive the boat."

Wow, the letter had made it through!

And Barker had taken it, at least the first brown envelope! So, he'd probably been seriously hoping to learn more.

The signal had been conveyed. Now what? Would it be like a game of tennis with the journalist? Well, the ball is in my court's side, Jo said to himself, thinking of his own tennis playing, another sport he liked much. Did Mandy play it?

***

It was 6 o'clock at the DD. A Friday night, June 11th

Jonathan expected a packed crowd. He was right.

At 6, it was almost full. The table on the upper level was already sequestered by the Chechen.

The two tables on the lower level were also occupied by businessmen who were close to drunk.

Two New England guys ran in, sat at the bar. Golfers, probably.

Wearing caps that extolled in red, "Boston Tee Party." Jo noticed immediately the tee-word, and not tea.

— Hi guys! What can I do for you?

- No taxation without representeeeeetion, one said with a pronounced, obvious drawl, forced.
- Live free or die, said the other.
- Yeah, New Hampshire? Offered Jo.
- Yep, that's where I'm from. This joker golfer is from Boston. We will take two fine B-52s and then a Cookanee.
- Don't have any Cookanee beer. Want to replace that with something else, my friends?
- Sure, a Heineken will do.
- Okay! Two Danish for the New England representatives! Coming right up!

Before the upper-level table cleared, Jonathan went over to speak with the clients at the lower-level one, so he could better catch snippets. He did pick up disturbing sentences portions.

The Chechen was explaining things to his table companions.

- Suez Canal charges heavy taxes... may open some containers. Unless you know the best hours. And the guy. Bribe heavy.
- No such trouble in Gdansk...
- but big road problems to Gdansk...
- Anatoly the Chechen likes the road, not planes nor trains, and does not trust the Russian guys, but he uses them often, no choice here, use a few of these Turkish guys too... solid as we need.

Anatoly the Chechen was talking about himself in the third person, as Caesar. Interesting enough.

— When are the arms leave Smolensk?
— Expecting Thursday, the 18th. Around 4:15 p.m., by truck, yeah, a few trucks. Four hours max to load. Surprise the two guards at breaktime. They take a small lunch and aren't usually careful. They should be, but twenty years without nothing happening relaxed their standards, and... well, you know; they're not careful anymore. Gerry intends to be at their favorite bar, will pay in vodka and beers... yeah, they may not even return to the warehouse in the afternoon. But this plan, uh-uh, not so sure.
— Already tried it?
— Sure. A few times. It worked. They now know a bit of Gerry; they think he's a kind of US guy turned into a new local contractor, paying tourneys to guys in the bar once in a while. Many Russians do, and strangers too. Gerry speaks a not so bad Russian. Or, if this doesn't work, we will make them open and kill them on site if needed. But to be seen.

Jo missed a lot of the conversation, but heard a good deal, as well. They appeared to be discussing a kind of plan A, plan B, plan C...

— Okay. So, we have to get the trucks?
— Yep. And you gotta hurry it up, guys. Five trucks, with one small Clark's lift in each, pallets, ropes,

hooks on the truck walls, and the like. Need 130 Kohn and Willy container small boxes, filled with scrap metal, similar weight as the arms boxes and containers, to replace the real ones in the warehouse. Could give us several more days. Have to do it quick, clean.

He kept on.

— The five trucks drivers will be staying outside, and they can't get a whiff of the content. Load fast. You need two very quick young guys, find the best in the region on the Clark propane forklifts; driven sitting, then kill them and thrown them into the Dnieper, cement blocks on their feet, you know the refrain. Or, better, keep them if you prefer them later for transboarding with the lift. I should be on site. But in case I can't make it, you know.
— Okay. Clean job. And then, we have to go to...

But the rest was swallowed up in the noise from lower table. Still, Jo clearly had enough info for a second brown envelope to Barker.

Back at the bar, with a big order from a few other clients, he was in a rush and didn't want the boss to hassle him.

— Here are your drinks, he said to those at the table on the lower level.

Guys at the table on high waved him over for beers. They kept talking.

— Prince Marty wants it for the 27th. All of it. One shot. No misses.
— Where? Where does he want it?
— First, get to the place I told you... call this place X for now. Have your false US, Ukrainian, and Russian passports, money in US dollars for the guys at the warehouse and other bribes, just in case. But it should work, and they will not talk.
— Okay. How much?
— $20,000 each. That's the A plan. Pay half in advance when you get on-site. Show them then the second $10,000 and promise it at the end of the unload. They'll open the doors. Two doors. Talk about their wives and children, mention where they live. If there's no kind of ease, or you have any doubts, kill them after opening and closing. But try not to kill them before the last truck leaves. Anyway, this is a plan, as I said. But everything can go wrong on site. Be ready to adapt.
— We throw them into the Dnieper, then, if we kill?
— Maybe, maybe not. There's a dump you'll pass, two miles away or so. Stop for a piss. Shoot them in the head, then in the face for harder identification, then bury them quickly under the garbage. If they go into the Dnieper and are later found, there'll be links the police will make with the Clark guys, and then, us.
— Yep. Got it.
— And what about our pay?

— The usual rate for one clean kill. Plus $25,000 each if the trucks reach the X place, with all the stuff. Now, let's all shut up and enjoy the booze.

Jonathan knew he was really in a skunk's hollow. Far, far deeper than he'd thought.

At 2 a.m., two half-drunk guys came in, one wearing a T-Shirt that had sprawled over the front, "Happy people are hiding something." Jonathan smiled.

— So, you're hiding what? This one asked.
— All kinds of drinks, mixes, and the cash, of course, Jonathan added.
— Lol, so unhide us two Grasshoppers, man. With a beer too? He glanced over at his buddy.
— Okay, but one with 0.5 alcohol one, said the buddy. I had enough alcohol, already. Say a Coors light, very light.
— Great! Coming up!

They had an accent, maybe from Arizona. But this time Jonathan wasn't at all sure. He had travelled all across USA and biked it widely, but all accents were, of course, not always so easy to distinguish. He needed keywords.

He thought for a second about that idea of getting everyone to go in on a round of a kind of test "*Guess my Accent!*" game.

3 a.m. Time to close up. Tired, distraught. He was back home now, and with a lot of dollars in tips! An unbelievable Friday. He would seriously have to talk to an accountant, soon, figure out his taxes. Then, a possibly quieter job, teaching economics in, say, New Orleans, San Francisco, or

Miami. Or in Montreal. Or here in NYC. And get a small summer home in Richford, maybe? Mom's idea was tempting. But he knew, somehow, he couldn't do this before this particular chapter of his life was closed.

Now, go on for Gerry and Anatoly's plans.

Not one of the two guys with the Chechen were on Billy's list.

They were probably Americans. Dangerous killers, probably.

Jo prepared a second envelope for Barker.

***

It went like this.

Two billion in arms from the ex-USSR at stake— hundreds of thousands of people could be killed.
Stage 2.

Mr. Barker, thanks for adding that comment about "**Uncertain Seas**." Events are rushing us to this point.

We now know that arms are leaving Smolensk on June 18th around noon. Five trucks will be loading them. We don't know the exact location of the warehouse. Somewhere around Smolensk, but no more info, sorry.

We don't have sure hints about where the trucks will go after that. The trucks will be carrying their own small Clarks lifts. As for the two lift operators, they could be killed and anyone who comes into contact with them. What could help you is that they have to find two excellent lift operators in Smolensk, or thereabouts. They said they will stop into a dump near the drop-off, two miles away, we picked up, probably bury the wardens and maybe lift guys there. So, if I were you, I would try to identify a dump close to the Dnieper. The warehouse should be near there.

He kept on.

The arms are going to be dropped off in a specific place, called X (we didn't get the name). Then on to Africa somewhere, by boat, we think. Don't know if it'll be by the Black Sea then to Suez Canal, or by Riga, Gdansk, St. Petersburg, White Sea... don't have these details.
The buyer's name we heard is Prince Marty. As for the where and why, we don't know yet. But the quantity of arms could justify a major revolution, or a big operation as Darfur, Congo or so. But not necessarily there. If you still believe us, please write "Chess Game" somewhere in your next article.
Another brown envelope should reach you by then with any other information we get. Don't worry, we don't want money, just more peace and justice across this messy planet, and a reduction in arms, violence, rapes, killings, children soldiers, poverty. And, of course, better education and a better world for all. All this is anonymous of course.
Yours truly, Jo the Pigeon.

***

He went to the NYT office, used another tourist to deliver the letter to Barker. This time, he had to pay $40. Nothing came cheap in Manhattan.

On Saturday, June 12th, Jo went to work and was greeted by no murky visitors. Sadly, though, no more info for him about the crooks' plan.

***

Sunday morning, June 13th, 9:30. Jonathan woke up, took a shower.

He had breakfast, which included some fair-trade coffee, one light muffin, some strawberries in yogurt.

He listened to the news. How he missed Vermont's NPR! No way to get that local radio station here. He made his lonesome way to his computer and to the web.

Humm, the New York Times. So, let's have a look at Barker's column, shall we?

There it was: Barker, with a follow-up on the Big Apple municipal affair. The mayor could be resigning. It was getting worse for him. At the end of the article… Eureka!

"The mayor should not be playing this kind of **chess game** with citizens' taxes and their minds. He should be providing us with more details, very soon. All citizens are invited to send us detailed information."

It was a clear message. A third brown envelope was needed, ASAP. But with what more in it this time?

The phone rang. Mom.

— Hello, is she nice? Your dad is already asking, since you never give us any news.
— Hello Mom, let's keep it quiet for now, please. How's Dad?

— Oh, I touched a nerve! Dad's fine, apparently enjoying his work with his small Massey Ferguson tractor.
— Maybe he really works, maybe! Can I call you around 12? Tell Dad not to forget to check the oil and all liquid levels in this old animal.
— Okay. I'll tell him. As if he needs this advice. Hope we'll know her name soon!

He managed to say he would call later in the day.

***

The third brown envelope. Jo used the list, mainly. Billy was not bad about Prince Marty the Third.

Two billion arms from the ex-USSR at stake— hundreds of thousand people could be killed. Stage 3.

Mr. Barker, please forgive me if my sentences are not entirely semantically perfect. Urgency speaks louder.

Buyer should be Prince Marty the Third. Residences: Five we are aware of. And, certainly more unknown, or temporary ones. Impossible to know which one is his favorite or most often used, and where he is now.

First, in Istanbul, Turkey. Second, in Geneva, Switzerland. Third, in Khartoum Sudan. Fourth, in New York. Fifth, in Moscow, Russia, located two houses away, on the same street of the Moscow mayor's residence, one mile away from the Moscow City Hall.

Prince Marty is suspected of all kind of trades, but officially making money with legal import-export, oil and gas, mining operation and fine arts. Age: 51. Born in Sudan. Polygamous. Probably between 10 to 30 children, 3 with favorite wife. Studied in three Universities, South Africa, Mozambique and Australia. We have not much more on him.

Prince Marty wants to receive all the stuff, on June 27th. Don't know where, nor how, but probably by boat.

Talk to you soon. Please use the keywords "Hands shake" in your next column.

Jo the pigeon. Still with you.

***

He returned the call to his mother.

— Mom, it's me.
— Yes, Jonathan, I know your voice. What was so urgent this morning that you couldn't talk to me?
— We'll discuss it later, don't worry.
— When are you visiting us? Is this bar job still serious?
— Yes, it is still. But I'm only off Mondays and Tuesdays.

He knew this wouldn't be a mere walk on the beach. Not available on weekends! Mom would be mortified. As for Dad.

— So, we'll have to visit the Apple, Dad and I, she said. If not, we kind of lose you? We are getting old. How long will this strange job last?
— Humm, could be months, maybe years. Mom, I really don't know. It's good pay, I like it, and…
— But what about your studies? Gone with the wind?
— I'll use what I learned, in managing my money.
— Okay, great idea! On Marvin, you know, Marvin Road, and on Pleasant View road, there are two gentlemen farmer's houses and lots for sale. Many New Yorkers have country houses, no?
— Which ones? Smith's property? Old Carey's? The O'Hara's at the top of Pleasant View?
— Yes, Norman O'Hara is ill, and not young anymore. He's 76, often at the Burlington hospital, even visiting hospitals in Montreal or Boston at times. Cancer. His wife's already dead, as you know, and his children working in Columbus, in Ohio. They want to sell, at least after Norman passes away, maybe now. I still like him. We exchange seeds every spring. He'd certainly be open to talking with you, instead of any stranger. Maybe now, before he dies, he might need money for the treatments, I don't know. Smith and Carey, they always say a right price could buy them. You never know. Would you offer a honest price?
— Hmm, Mom, give me a few weeks, okay? I'll come out. But tell Mr. O'Hara I could be interested.
— Promises, promises.
— No, I'm serious. It is a good idea to have a country house close to you, even if I work far. Could go

many times a year, holidays, week-ends, yep. Say hi to Dad. I love him. And you, of course.
— Great. Talk to you soon. Say hi to your new girlfriend whom we don't know. Eat your carrots.

Mom will always be mom… eat your carrots! He smiled.

Jo had a message, on voicemail. Amanda. Rather, Mandy, as he was now thinking of her.

The message: "Please call when you can, busy man." Short and sweet.

— Hello, young Asian-European lady.
— Yes, how are you, Green Mountain muchacho?
— Ready for a bike ride? To Bleecker Street?
— Okay, good idea! You seem full of them.
— But I have to leave a package before, okay?
— A package?
— Yes. But I'll see you at the same corner, at 1 this afternoon?
— I work at 6, you know.
— Yes, I know, killer bartender of these lonely hearts' club bands.

Humm, things were getting serious with Mandy. A rather clear message from her, not a very difficult code to crack, these words from the Beatle's album.

He got dressed. It was a nice day. 76 Fahrenheit degrees, a nice breeze, sunny, mid-June.

He biked to the Times with the envelope.

- Hi, sir, would you like to make twenty bucks right now?
- Who wouldn't?
- No scam. Ten dollars if you leave this envelope in the NY Times office right there, and ten bucks, after, when you get back.
- No bomb? The guy said, laughing.
- No bomb, no anthrax, only info about the mayor.
- Maybe another kind of bomb, then? Yes sir, I'll do it. The mayor we have now has to go! Bring out the tenser, first, please.
- Here you go.

The guy went in, came back, took the second 10, and left. Then things went odds.

- I want a 10 dollars bill too, Amanda said.
- Mandy, oh... what... what... are you doing here, you kind of spy on me? Jo said.
- I am here purely by coincidence. I found some fine chocolates for you right there, minutes ago, and saw you when I got out. What's that scam? She said, half amazed, half serious.

Jo was hesitating. To be or not to be. To talk or not to talk. To risk or not to risk. She saw the hesitation.

- I will guess. You don't like the mayor and responded to the Barker request for info!
- Yes. Let's walk this way with the bike, he said.

— But why give the envelope to the guy? What was in the envelope? I saw you, so don't try to squirm out of this one.
— Humm... I'm easily identifiable... you don't know what the mayor can do, later, if he is forced to resign.
— You're inventive, dreamy boy. I do not want to spend my time with a guy fearing the CIA and NSA every minute, about a mayor, she said, a little more seriously this time. Though I know these things exists.
— I will have to talk more to you about this, maybe.
— Not maybe, she ventured. When?
— Well, I'm off tomorrow. And the weather forecast says it's supposed to be fine, sunny, not windy. Are you off too?
— Yes, totally free for two days. What do you have in mind, she asked, clearly interested in the two days mention, and a little nervous, as they started to ride toward Washington Park, and the Bleecker street area. You look like a Chevalier Teuton, fighting the mayor!
— The Chevaliers Teutons were tough fighters in Germany, or rather Prussia, I think.
— Yes, Prussia, in the Middle Ages.
— I'm not one. But I have something in mind for these two days, maybe. Would you be interested (this part was tougher... so he slowed down), in a two-day trip in the Catskills?
— Like... with a group? She asked, roguishly.
— Yes, with a group.

— How many people, she mumbled, in this "group"?
— Humm, would be a small group.
— But how many people, she persisted, apparently upset about having to be in a group.
— Humm, the kind of two. You and me.
— You got me, wonderful! As a smile sun-shined her face. I have a Schwinn ready for hills and some dirt roads? As for the other conditions, I don't mind. You take care of them.
— Fine, he said, at a heartrate of 200 beats a minute.

Bleecker Street was, as usual, nice and clean, people walking, stopping at small historic houses.

It was so colorful on this street, with flowers on balconies, everywhere.

They left their bikes attached to one post and started to walk around.

She took his hand and kept it for one hour.

Her hair was floating in the light wind, under the sun.

They kept sneaking glances at one another, smiling, turning into streets as they came to them. They both knew Manhattan reasonably well, and so, knew they did not get too far from the bikes.

They didn't talk much. Amanda didn't ask about the envelope, and he didn't say anything more about it.

They both knew the other one was daydreaming, so they let things be as they were.

***

Sunday night, June 13th.

At the DD, Jonathan had to admit he had been thinking of Mandy, all the time.

Maybe he wasn't as attentive to clients, signs, and consequently lost some tips.

But he didn't care too much. And, fortunately, the boss wasn't in. Still, he watched the key tables.

At 7:45, the Chechen entered, with Gerry.

Of course, they immediately walked in the direction of the table on the upper level.

Unfortunately, for them, it was occupied. Smiling, Gerry reached into his pocket and offered money to the three women seated there to move to the table on the lower level. Nothing new for him.

Jonathan was looking, discretely. The women accepted.

Two government workers walked slowly to the bar, still sober. One wore a cap with a wide inscription, "I used all my sick days, so I called in: DEAD."

— What can I do for the dead guy? Jonathan asked.
— Bring us a "cold" drink! The one with the cap joked.
— What kind?
— Two chilled Holland Grolschs.
— Okay, good suggestion. With a big cheese chunk, or chunks, maybe.
— Chunks, yes. Big chunks, we don't do. Sounds too much like throw up. Huge, I do.
— So, huge chunks, yep.
— Great! I'll go in back, milk a cow and come back in an hour, Jonathan joked.

They laughed and continued some conversation they'd been having on the school system in the Netherlands.

Jo went over to the table with the women who'd pocketed the bribe, asked what he could get them. He was well situated again to overhear the Chechen and Gerry (only the two of them this time), the Chechen talking and apparently not in a rush to ask for beers, as was usual.

— Hi, ladies! Where are you from?
— Guess.
— Okay. I'll need a few clues, please. What kind of jobs or jokes do you have, he asked, placing napkins on the table.
— I'm dentist; she's a nurse. Our parents went to Indiana, when they were young, and lived there a while. I studied there. I have two dogs, no horse, no crocodile, no pig.
— But your accent doesn't sound like it's from Indiana, at first glance… or first hear, I mean, he added with a wink.
— Right, she retorted. I said, "studied in Indiana." Not born there.

The other woman took up her napkin. They both talked more.

— I like football. Texas Cowboys for me, and she prefers the Green Bay Packers. Dad's a fan of the Tennessee Oilers, my brother too. Mom and the rest of my family have been sold to the San Francisco 49ers, ever since Joe Montana's years. I loved Bret

Favre, but there's no one I really idolize. They earn too much.
— Okay, I've got enough now to guess the accents.

He pointed to the first lady with his chin.

— For you, I guess Ohio, and for her Kentucky, or southern Illinois, or, well, I'd say somewhere close to either one or a combo of the four borders of Kentucky, Illinois, Tennessee and Missouri. In that general area.
— You're a genius! She seemed ecstatic. I'm from Cincinnati. My friend here's from Kentucky, both in the region you described. How do you get the accents so well?
— Pure luck, he smiled. No, in fact, I simply heard a lot, a lot of them, people I met while studying were from all across USA. Often, the way one or two keywords are pronounced, or an expression, really help. What'll it be for you two? What can I get you to drink?
— Not pure luck, indeed! Impossible. We'd like two beers, any kind, as long as it's on-tap, please.
— Any kind on-tap? Okay! I'll be back in a moment. Have fun.

He'd managed this time to catch a good deal of the conversation at the table on the upper level this time, while talking with the ladies. A horrible one. Terrifying, even though he'd missed a lot of what they were saying.

— For the 18th, things are okay? Asked the Chechen.
— Yes. Then we've got to settle the second part, and third.
— Second part... trucks will sleep in a small unknown town in the Ukraine, probably (a name badly pronounced, so Jo wasn't sure what had been said at this point). Then, low risk until Odessa. Or Sevastopol, in Crimea.
— Why Sevastopol? It's much farther, and through the mountains.
— Other Chechens on-site will tell us. Plan may change every day, you know. People switch jobs, turn their coats. Gas-Prone makes many calls. Then, they go back to Moscow or Kiev, disappear, are killed or maimed. Their children are kidnapped; then they pay their ladies to leave for Switzerland, Italy... to be silent. They do anything.
— Okay, then, the Black Sea. When, how?
— With the Grey Shark boat or the Isaacson: either one will be there. It will reach the port, pick up the loads, and sail to Istanbul, then to Prince Marty. After a port on the Black Sea, the plan should not, under any circumstance whatsoever, change. Only before this point can it change.
— Well, Marty's still far away, can we act without being sure?
— Yes, that's what I'm paid for, paid every week, and you are too, I imagine?
— Yes. And well paid, I should say. Went with some bonuses, at times.

- Me too. So, this is the proof. We may not know all before Istanbul.
- Waiter! Two vodkas on ice. And hurry!

Jonathan served them.
They left at 10.
So, he reasoned they'll go first by the easiest, shortest way. This is what he'd thought at start: first, by the Black Sea, then to Istanbul, then through the Suez Canal and finally ending up somewhere in Africa.

But the bandits still appeared not to know exactly how they'd get from Smolensk to the Black Sea by trucks.

***

10:30, Sunday night, June 13

A tall black gentleman of about thirty went in, sat down, and motioned to Jo behind the bar.

- Hi. A Sudanese beer please.
- Excuse me, sir, but we don't have any.
- You should sell some.

Jonathan smiled.

- I'm not so sure. In fact, Sudan, I think the Sudanese government doesn't permit the production of alcohol on its soil, officially, at least!
- Then, you don't know about Sudan. I do. We do import the Bell, Club and Nile Special, at least, and those Ugandan lagers beers, and more.

— Oh, sorry, sir. I wasn't aware. So, I have, for sure, several Nile Specials.

Jonathan noted the word "we" in the man's sentence: so, he was from Sudan.

— Then, a Nile Special will certainly do! For starters, that is.

Jonathan served him his Nile Special, then went on to serve several other tables, and returned.

— Another one.
— Okay. Another Nile Special?
— Yep. So, tell me: what else do you know about Sudan?

Jonathan played defense. Better be safe than sorry. He did not know to who he was talking to.

— Not much more than what I told you. I heard that recently, you know, or read it in the news, don't remember. A huge country, but what else.
— Which newspaper, or, was somebody here, discussing with you about Sudan?

The guy turned around on his stool. Looked everywhere.

— Was anyone here talking about the region?

He was too insistent, too curious.

- You know, I'm only a bartender. I hear things being said, overhear, maybe mix things up a bit. I don't really care conservation, only serving to my best.
- But you were quite right: there was stuff coming out from Sudan, the latest news. Where did you get all this information?
- Honestly, I don't remember. A question, maybe, in the most recent version of Trivial Pursuit? Or a Jeopardy hint from Alex Trebek? You know, my job is to have people just talk, have fun. I simply jump into their favorite subject, even if I know almost nothing about it.
- Ha, ha! Maybe, the guy said, looking a little more relaxed.
- It's true, you're only a bartender, after all.

He was drinking quickly and didn't tip. Not very polite, but well dressed, and with an international English, very slight to no accent.

- I'll take another beer, this time a Three Elephants if by miracle you have.
- Yes sir, good news, we do indeed store this one.

He looked at ease but said nothing. Five minutes later, the first of the Three Elephants was gone. He took the second right away. Jonathan didn't say anything, but he knew that this draught was from Mozambique: a country not unknown to Jonathan. For one year, in Burlington, he'd studied econometrics with a guy from the capital, Maputo.

So, four beers in 17 minutes, noted Jonathan the economist.

— Now, I will have a Stinger, man. A very good drink for the wealthy.
— Made with brandy and white crème de menthe, shaken and in a cocktail glass? Asked Jonathan, since he knew many versions of this cocktail.
— Yes. A triple, please.
— Everybody here is rich or looks or says so, in so many words. But many of them drink beer, said Jo.
— You know what "big rich" means? I mean, richer than that.
— Nope.

He pointed to himself. He was getting drunk, obviously.

— Since you are only a bartender, I can tell you who I am. You won't believe it, not in many years!
— Well, I may not. So, I can definitely take it, said Jonathan, smiling, extremely curious.
— I'm Prince Marty.

Commotion in Jo's head.

Although he'd of course noticed the name on the list, when Billy had collapsed, he'd been mentioning it, and Jo had of course overheard the crooks talking about this guy, the buyer of $2 billion's worth of arms.

Despite all this, Jonathan hadn't seen it coming. He kept his composure, looked casually under the bar, and said a few words.

— Prince Martin?
— Not Prince Martin, but Prince Marty. Marty the Fourth.

This was even less expected. Jonathan was unable to talk for a moment. Then, he tried something clumsy, while getting a glass from the rack over his head.

— Where and how old are the Marty I, II and III?
— None of your business, but they are rich, as am I. And this is what is important, Prince Marty IV said, draining his Stinger.

He was now talking much, but not so clearly. On a lot of things.

Four beers and a triple Stinger was equivalent to maybe eight times a normal beer, and the Prince had downed all that in 40 minutes. Clearly, he was not taking care in what he said, and since only a bartender could hear it, whatever 'it' was, he took another Stinger. A double, this time.

— So, that's me. That is I. I am Prince Marty the Fourth, yes. And I will make more money than my father. More than every other family member. Peter the Great went to Holland, to England, everywhere in Europe to modernize Russia in 1700, or thereabouts, with genius maritime engineers in tow,

along with his party friends. And then he built St. Petersburg and the harbor. I will (he hesitated a little) visit all America and the World to see how oil and bullets can bring me power.
— What did you say? Jo asked, as casual as he could, as he was preparing a Brazilian coffee.
— Nothing important, Marty said. Bring me a last Stinger. A single this time.
— Ok, if you need a cab, sir, let me know. It is late.
— Cab? Nah, my driver has my limo outside.

At midnight, Marty IV was gone. Completely drunk. Jonathan was quite sure the Prince would not remember much of what he'd said. Back at the apartment, he was wealthier in a way, with $725 of tips, but nothing from Marty the rich imperial man. He wrote Part 4 of his letters for the brown envelopes, about Marty, oil, bullets, power, money. Since he and Amanda were leaving to go to the Catskills on Monday at 8 am, he had to find a way to deliver it before then.

The Catskills

Monday, June 14, 9.15

Jonathan left the fourth brown envelope to Barker, the way he did before.

The content was everything and approximately what Jonathan knew concerning Prince Marty the Fourth: age, height, and, mainly, that he existed and could be involved in the big purchase.

Could.

He asked Barker to use the words "Looking drunk" in one of his next two columns.

Jo would try to read it in the Catskills, if not, in New York when they got back from their two days bike escape.

He went to Amanda's apartment to meet her and go. At 9:45, as expected, they were ready to start.

- You have all you need in these two small luggage pieces? He asked.
- Not everything. I still have to get the bike bag to put on my rack. Here it is.
- Great! So, we're ready to leave. I rented a car, with two bikes spots on the back rack, rented too.

They had a deep conversation in the vehicle.

Amanda probably did not want to wait too long with the brown envelop, and would ask to get back if not satisfied with his answers, he thought.

One hour later, they were closer to the Catskills.

— Jonathan, you know I like your companionship, but I'm still not totally convinced you told me the truth, all the truth, nothing but the truth about these envelopes.

She laughed.

— Ever since I saw you with this one brown envelope, and you handed it over. And I may even doubt your Economics diplomas.

She said this portion half-smiling, half-threatening. He took in a long breath.

Okay, listen Amanda, please. First, let me explain some things about economics.

He went through an 8 minutes discussion on math, stats, econometrics, elasticity of demand and supply, Gross National Product, the whole list of courses required for a Bachelor's degree in Econometrics, details of economic development, Gini's coefficients, IDH, and many other indices per country, the role of the FED, and so on.

She stopped him.

— Master, I have enough! I believe you on point one. Now, point 2, the envelope, the mayor, and what else?
— This is more complicated. Much more. I don't know if I should.
— Then, let's go back if you don't talk. I don't want to bike with a half-crook.
— Okay.

This time, he decided to go for broke.

He told her about Billy's collapse, the USB key, the list, everything up to the brown envelope.

— If you get scared, or don't like, we can go back. Just ask.
— No, I'm not at all scared. You know, even international bandits may be and should be checked and denounced by ordinary citizens, when possible. You shoot info to top police, or the newspapers, or… Billy's list? What kind of list?

Fantastic. So, he thought, she's becoming an ally, too, in this new, risky business he's gone into. Maybe she's a magic muse.

This time he dove in for good.

— A list of names, with first names, family names, professions, revenue, and many other details, some photos. Many of these guys on the list come into the DD for murky business. I identified many of them.
— Where is that list?

— Here.

He reached into his purse and took out a few sheets, then showed her a partial, short, printed version.

— Okay. And I see what you're saying, some of them come at the DD. But how do you know about their murky business?
— Acoustics.
— Acoustics?
— Yes.

He explained the sound effects of the area, the upper-level table and lower-level tables.

— Don't know how, but it works. Perhaps it's like the Ancient Greek theater.
— And you were spying on them, while talking to me, is this what you mean?
— Humm, yes. I... had to serve you, no? And when you flashed me that oh-so-beautiful smile, I couldn't do much else but stay at your table a while longer. So, what about the service?
— Top notch. Very personalized, too, she said, looking into his eyes. But, sorry, keep staring at the road, good-looking bartender. You're driving a car. So, is there more?
— Much more.

They were now in the Catskills. The road had narrowed and now curved, made its way uphill, then down, ended its poetic wandering in the woods. Beyond, often, the lakes shone splendidly.

— What a beauty, these mountains, Amanda said. Is there a town nearby?
— Yes. A small city. Plenty of hills, uncrowded roads. We can get lost anywhere.
— You mean, half-lost? She hinted.
— I'd say 40% lost, just enough to get back, I mean.
— Great! And where will we sleep? She risked.
— Gigi's Bed and Breakfast. I reserved two rooms. Adjacent.
— Two rooms… adjacent, of course, she repeated, smiling.
— But adjacent is a good idea, I think. In case I want to talk to you about these brown envelopes and the list, I won't be too far away.

He could dream, nothing wrong with that; so, he did, for a second.

— Keep those eyes on the road, Mr. Chauffeur. But tell me more about the list.
— Okay.

He detailed almost everything. Even risked telling her things about Prince Marty the Third, then the Fourth. She listened silently.

— I don't know anything about these princes, she said. But I do know that, regularly, arms are going through the Bosporus and Dardanelles Straits in Turkey and that they bypass the Istanbul checkpoints there. Usually, they come from Transnistria, a kind of lawless, fake republic, kept up almost only for the production of arms, by God knows who, Russia perhaps. And then the arms go to Russia indeed, but also to the Mediterranean, then to the final destination, the one to use them, across the world.

— Where is Transnistria?

— A region located between Moldova and Ukraine. Maintained exactly by who knows, but probably the Russian government closes its eyes to all this. Or supports, or even finance.

— But this time we're talking about possibly much more?

— Yes, if what you say is to be believed. And Smolensk is a terribly murky place, ever since the 30s. Stalin liked to have murders take place there. Same old, same old, probably. All of what you heard these bandits say is totally plausible, as far as I'm concerned.

Mandy was pretty good informed about illegal trades, what an amazing fact, he thought.

They had reached the B&B around noon and registered.

The man at the front looked at each of them, smiled, and said that they had, in fact, two vacant, small, single rooms, adjacent.

— Two rooms? The clerk asked, with a bemused look. Good for our business. And I get twice the tip, I hope, he joked.
— Depends on service, Jonathan said, smiling.
— And discretion, Amanda whispered, looking out of the corner of her eye, head tilted, turned to Jonathan, who melted.

In the rooms, they left their bags and went outside to unstrap the bicycles. They'd brought a lunch, so they decided to have a picnic. A beautiful site, lost in the hills. At 12:30, they went biking, intending to be back for the B&B's dinner at 7:30.

— I wanted to optimize the time we have for sport. As you know, it's mid-June, and the solstice is on June 21st, so these are the longest days of the year, he said.
— No. Rather, the longest periods of possible sunshine, she clarified. All days are 24 hours, as far as I know, she joked.
— Sure, señora profesora. Let's ride.

They started on a flat road section, four miles. Then they took a narrow dirt road, along a brook, heard the noise of the fresh, clean water drifting along the rocks, and climbed for the next two miles. They rode a few hours, discussing more of the things Jo already knew about the Marty's, the outlaws, the list, but, principally, about the beautiful nature surrounding them.

They finished biking almost at 4:30 on the dot. Took a shower, changed clothes, and were back at 6, in a small reading room. They had a romantic discussion and a fine dinner. Amanda suggested Billy was a blackmailer. Jo angled toward the CIA.

At 9, they went to bed.

— Good night.
— Good night.

At 9:05, Amanda knocked at the door; Jonathan answered.

— Yes?
— It's a little cold, in my room; how's yours? I don't understand how the heating works in mine... even in June, high in these hills, it's a chilly night...
— It seems working okay here in mine, he said, a little shaky.
— May I compare?
— Yes... yes, he mumbled. Give me 30 seconds, and I'll prepare a kind of wall, with two pillows to separate us.
— Great idea. 30 seconds, not more.

15 seconds later, she dove under his blankets, and the fake pillow wall vanished.

***

On Tuesday morning, the clerk and the owner were present and saw the love in their eyes.

They recommended some roads to take with their bikes.

Both lovers thought the suggested roads had too much traffic: cars, motorcycles and some small delivery trucks.

And they weren't at all difficult enough. But they were really interested in making the journey at least partly on dirt roads.

— You may leave the car here, ride, and come back at any time you want. Sunset is around 8:30 pm here, but real dark later, could I say.
— Thanks. We should be here around 6. Then we have to get back to the city, avoiding traffic, and say, in Manhattan around 9.
— These Manhattan guys, always on the rush. Have a nice day!

They biked, discussed the crooks' plans again, got lost in the beautiful hills and woods.

They also talked how Amanda could be involved in the project. Jonathan didn't want there to be any risk for her. She proposed she'd be a kind of researcher, on the web, calling Istanbul maybe, and so on.

Back in Manhattan, Amanda asked if better to stay in Jonathan's apartment for the night. Jonathan suggested that he would go to hers, instead. Prudence. Less likely that your apartment is checked than mine.

True, she agreed. They had a wonderful night, short on sleep, full of love.

***

Wednesday morning, June 16, 7 a.m.

Mandy had to go to work. Jonathan left for his apartment. He went on the web, pulled up the news. Barker's columns, to be precise.

Yes, he'd used the keyword "Handshake".

I still need more info, Jonathan thought. He tried to see what was up abroad about their case, too.

In the Moscow Times, he read about actions of the Moscow mayor and the federal government, apparently against corruption. Nothing new, words only or real moves? Not sure.

In the Ukrainian newspapers: problems with the education system, river level higher than usual, and the soccer national team lost the game against Estonia, a weak team since many years. A shameful unexpected 5-1 defeat. Betting on soccer games was a heavy source of revenue, legal and illegal, in Ukraine. The goalkeeper was particularly bad, mainly on two normally easy free kicks. He did not settle the defensive wall correctly, so the attacking team, Estonia, scored twice on low quality shots. And a third goal on a bad rebound he gave on a rather routine shot, just in front of the net. The Ukrainian key forwards fired seven times over the net, some from normally good spots to score. *Humm,* Jonathan thought. *Fixed games?*

Then, in a small column, apparently of low importance, he saw something about a potential strike yet to happen at the harbors, in Odessa and Kherson, Ukraine.

Government employees checking the contents of containers, among other things, were not satisfied with their working conditions.

They would be on strike on Sunday, for as long as needed. In the city of Kherson, and in Odessa, both on the Black Sea! Did a strike meant weaker or no control over the loading and unloading of containers?

Could Anatoly and Gerry offer money, ostensibly to help the workers but in fact to foment the strike? Yep, sure.

He pulled up the World Bank website, and several other ones. The UN website.

The Blue Helmets were missing money. Refugee camps in Chad were overcrowded.

Darfur still a messy place; Chinese oil companies were playing a strange role there.

The Swedish government was voting on new credits for education and increasing the higher income tax rate percentage bracket.

France was going to be "helping" in Ivory Coast, but didn't say how.

Not much more that was interesting concerning Russia, Ukraine, Belarus or even Turkey, that day.

At 5:30, he called Amanda. They had agreed not to talk about the "project" on the phone, nor too much about their relationship, for that matter.

— Hello, Turkish queen! How was your day?
— Fine, Vermont grand vizier, fine. And yours?
— As good as it can be, would have been a way brighter journey if spent entirely with you!
— Sure, same for me! You work at 6?

— Yes. Send me a text message, maybe.
— Okay. You know, I have my book club, tonight. Bye-bye. Take care.

At 6, he was at the DD.

On Wednesdays, they had a special Happy Hour on imported beers, from 5 to 8.

In fact, they varied the specials on a daily basis.

Business was running well, the customers were happy, the boss was happy, the waiters were happy.

Everything was looking good. Indeed, it was.

Two municipal contractors from Alabama, on Holidays in NYC, were exchanging views at the bar.

— Don't ask what you can do for your county, but ask what your county's elected rep can do for you!
— Hey, waiter, two beers, please.
— Sure. What kind?
— Humm, let's make them two Bud Lights.

They went to sit alongside the wall. Then, the Flint garbage guys entered. So, they were not dead!

— How are you guys? Asked Jonathan, waiting for them to talk about the gunfire they certainly witnessed out there, days ago.
— Still alive! Give us two gin and tonics. Did you hear the gunshots when we left last time?
— So, one thing first: I do not give anything away; you have to pay! Secondly, yes, I heard it. Even thought

you were hit by a lost bullet, or worse, targeted, by competitors maybe!
— Thanks, we'll of course pay! Yes, we were close to the shots. Very close. We saw a White guy, firing from a car; then the vehicle disappeared on the street corner. A man was dead. Another one wounded seriously. He died later, as far as we know from the news. Police went in seconds later. We moved away, you know, we were scared, and people were all around, but, well, we didn't stick on site and didn't see anything more. Please don't ask us to talk to the police; we don't want to buy us any trouble.
— I know nothing more, guys. Which is what I will say to the police, if they come back, that is. I'm only a bartender, you know.

Sure. One New York newspaper had mentioned the dead man was from Tanzania, but the article was not clear at all. Thanks God, the honest Flint guys were alive.

Finally, Wednesday night turned busy and stayed that way until 11:30, but everything went smoothly soon after. Jo closed early, at 1:30 in the morning. The boss watched there all evening, and only 5 clients were still left at 1.

But Jo was pretty pleased: $610 in tips. He really was a jewel, and the boss knew this. He was quick to prepare drinks and cocktails, had no miss in quantities, no complaints by clients, certainly not by women, and no errors in the cash counts.

And he was able to talk about any subject, smiling when needed, serious if required, too. It clearly increased the sales and client satisfaction.

Jonathan went to bed, happy with his day. At last, he felt being a bartender at the good ole DD was a good job. Why were Mom and Dad worrying, he would buy in Vermont soon, hopefully. Taking care of them in their old age, as much as he could.

***

Thursday, June 17

Amanda was working all day.

Jonathan went for a walk, after taking a look at the web. No interesting news that would help "the project."

At 6, he was back at his old haunts, the bar, ready for work. Around 7, Marty the Fourth popped up.

He sat at the bar, asking several questions. He wanted to verify if Jonathan remembered him, and key things he had said, perhaps.

Apparently satisfied with the vagueness of Jo's answers, he went to the upper-level table, took out his cell phone and dialed.

Ten minutes later, the Chechen joined him.

Two minutes after, the lower-level table was filled by two businessmen from California. Jonathan had to be prudent, he knew. Even more than usual, because of Marty IV. He went to serve these guys from San Diego (i.e. from California).

Three interesting words that came through from the key table at the upper level sounded like: "Soocatrah," "The

Zanza Bar," and something like "Pinim-ba," or "Pa-nemba." The three words weren't at all clear.

But he didn't want Marty to think he was listening, so he quickly served the Californians. Anyways, they had no time to lose with a bartender.

Back at the bar, he was pretty busy.

Thursday nights at the DD were usually very good; he had to be quick and on top of everything. If not, the boss would not appreciate, and his tips would be much lower. So, he had to stay away from the lower-level table, having too much work at the bar anyways. Marty would not suspect a thing.

Only one short visit to the lower-level table.

But these three strange words from Marty came back to his mind.

Three dudes entered, swaggered up to the bar. One wore a T-Shirt, with the expression on the front: "Life is full of disappointments. Just ask my parents."

— Hello, guys. Where are your happy parents?
— Hi, man. Oh, this shirt! I see. In New Orleans, since Katrina devastated everyone's home in 2005, and nobody paid for the damages. We will take 3 beers, Heinekens.
— Okay! And what about you, guys?
— I'm from Maine.
— From Delaware. We work here as city employees. We clean the streets, wash the mayor's cars, repair fire equipment. You know, stuff like that.
— The mayor, Jonathan said, trying to keep his smile down a notch. Will he survive this crisis?

— No. I hope not. This time, he went too far. Tomorrow, the New York Times and other newspapers will reveal heavy news. Millions and millions of dollars of contracts to Barry's Building Co. No tenders. Maybe 100 million of dark bread. We know it because some mafia guys have been drinking too much, and sometimes they talk to nobody's like us, blue collar workers.

The tallest one winked at his companion and Jo, and gently laughed.

— How come you know the New York Times will publish it? Said Jo.
— We are the leak to Barker! And it's not the first time.
— Wow! I'll definitely read it. Not sure to believe you yet, though!

They took their beers. They were right. The Times got it in the next day. A lot about Barry's Building Co.

The mayor was giving contracts without legal tenders to many little and bigger mafia groups, since years.

Amanda was right too. Ordinary people could change things, sometimes.

Jonathan closed late. 3:30 am. $850 in tips. Then, he read a few chunks, and, finally, he slept.

Dreaming of Amanda's visit, scheduled around 7:30, or before at her will.

***

On Friday morning, June 18, Amanda knocked at the door at 7.

Jonathan was still in pajamas but awake now that the bell had woken him.

He opened.

She rushed in, embracing him, kissing him slowly.

— How are you, honey? I missed you. This bike ride was the best thing I ever did.
— I agree, he said, as she was removing his pajamas.
— First things first, she whispered.
— Crooks later, he said.

Around 9:15, they went out to the kitchen, slowly.

— Coffee, dear Turkish lady?
— Yes, dear sultan, black, as our sea. You know I read a lot about it yesterday. The Kherson port is Swiss cheese, I mean, with so many holes, but not impossible they may be stopped there.
— Humm. There's a dock's workers strike going on there. I just read about it in the Ukrainian newspaper.
— Ah... then, they can now easily pass. You read Russian and Ukrainian?
— None. They have English versions. And the news about the strike was a very short article. I use Google translate.
— What do you think, then? She continued.
— I heard Marty the Fourth discuss something about the shipment with the Chechen at the DD yesterday.

— What a power couple!
— Yes. Very dangerous.

He had a flash. VD! That's what Billy's list meant, probably.

Others were ND, UK…

— ND: Not Dangerous, UK: from United Kingdom, or "UnKnown," maybe, said Jo.
— I would say "UnKnown," not United Kingdom, it seems to be the risk level of these guys.
— Indeed.

They looked at Billy's list.

Yep, ND would probably mean: Not Dangerous, VD for Very Dangerous. Okay, but why was it important for Billy? Still an open question. And Billy still in a coma, at latest news they had.

— Did you get hints on other important things?
— No, not much more. Oh, wait, maybe three strange, unclear words I remember from Marty's table.
— Which words? Mandy said.
— I heard something like "Soocatrah," then the "Zenza," "Zonza," or the "Zanza Bar." And even less clear was "Pinim-ba." or "Pa-nemba," or something like that.
— Let's look at a world map! You may have hit the jackpot.
— What do you think? I don't see what the hell these words could mean.

She looked at him, smiling.

— Are you serious? You don't see anything? She said.
— Well, I didn't find any bar that goes by the name of Zenza. And Soocatrah, Panimba or so, not sure I heard that right. No, I may be blind, but no.
— Well, it was noisy!

She smiled, then laughed a bit.

— Let me help you, we are a team, aren't we?

She opened a good old World Atlas Jonathan had on his shelf.

— Look here, pseudo-genius. This is what I understand from their words.

She pointed to the map. There it was: Socotra, not Soocatrah.

— Here's what they said, I think. Listen. Socotra is an island just off the extreme eastern point of the country of Somalia, on the Arabian Sea. You reach it by boat when you leave the Red Sea, pass the Bab-El-Mandeb Strait and the Gulf of Aden.
— Interesting! But what's the link with a bar called Zenza, in Manhattan or elsewhere?
— Stage 2. Not the Zanzabar, but Zanzibar, wonderful islands next to Tanzania: you know of it, I hope?

The Tanzania name comes from the merging of Tanganyika and Zanzibar. Got it? She winked.
— Yes, for sure I know! Didn't made the link, actually. So, the arms would be shipped to Africa, way after Istanbul, through the Suez Canal, the Red Sea, Socotra island, Zanzibar islands... that's possible! But what about Pinim-ba, or Pa-nemba or whatever it's called?
— Oh, for this one, I can't say, but you know what? Let's play the game of elimination, or reasoning, or let's take a break and come back to it a little later.
— Okay, let's take a break and think a bit.

They went outside, onto the balcony, breathed in some fresh air. Twenty minutes later, they returned to the sofa and to the brainstorm. He started.

— Can it be the name of a bandit? Or a surname, something more complicated.
— Maybe.
— One name of a minister; another's a prince, sheik; one's a mafia boss, a billionaire...
— Jonathan, try to remember exactly how he pronounced it and if there were any words before or after that could help us.
— Okay. Let's see. I think he said something, but badly pronounced, "Pinim-ba," or "Panemba" or even "Pa-emba" maybe.
— Okay, so let's do a search for a place, city, harbor whose name resembles those pronunciations, is that reasonable? The first two were locations, sites...

Socotra and Zanzibar, Amanda risked, her eyes on fire.
— Yep, go.

She took Jonathan's old World Atlas book again, then turned to the web and found pages detailing Africa coast south of Zanzibar, searched a long while, until she focused on the island of Madagascar and its surroundings.

— Got it, I think! She triumphed. Well, maybe. The city of Pemba, west of the Comoros islands, on the east coast of Mozambique, in the northern part of that country; population, 140,000, in 2007, Wikipedia says. Maybe a part of the shipment could go to Zanzibar, and a part to Mozambique through Pemba?

He was nervous. They probably had gotten it. They brainstormed and investigated a little more. He wondered out loud.

— What kind of port and region is Pemba in? Well, first, now the word and pronunciation really make sense. You know, sorry but I thought of Zanzabar as a bar.

She gently smiled at him and kissed him on the cheek.

— You're all forgiven. Not every person on this Earth knows where Zanzibar is or even knows it exists. Far less so for Pemba. It's not such a big port or big

city. But you know pirates, smugglers, and the mafia may prefer them. Lower controls, lower bribes to pay, less chance of a police investigation when killings are required upon delivering or uploading, maybe?
— I read something about the UN Security Council last week. They had to vote for credits on the Blue Helmets. In Mozambique, Chad, and elsewhere, but I don't remember exactly.
— Wow! It matches.

They went onto the UN website.

Yes, in fact a vote had been taken on whether or not there should be credits of $30 million to go toward Blue Helmets in Mozambique because of the difficult situation there.

The troops loyal to the actual "number two" in the government in the country were threatening a coup d'état. UN Blue Helmets were likely to intervene before, but the Security Council didn't get the majority vote.

Russia voted against.

At this point, Mandy and Jo went onto the site of the International Herald Tribune, then onto the New York Times site, next The Independent, then to Jeune Afrique, and Le Monde Diplomatique.

And they checked out more newspaper sites. Everyone seemed perplexed and didn't understand Russia's position. They all concluded, more or less, that it was just another "soap opera" of "tactics politics" to influence a decision elsewhere, indirectly, by blocking something Russia was not really concerned with. "Realpolitik."

— About Russia: it's not realpolitik! It may be about a major mafia smuggling or arms, but somebody, at a very high international level, probably knows about the Smolensk warehouse.

Mandy looked into Jonathan's eyes.

— And many other people, too, have to know, for a big operation like this? He offered.
— Not necessarily many. Very few may be aware of all details. Did you hear the bandits drop any big names?
— No.
— I'm saying, not necessarily, because the less people involved who know about the contents and about the operation, the more likely it will go ahead swiftly, the less people you have to manage and maybe kill, and the more money left at the end.
— Yes, but how many people, approximately, should know the whole story, do you think? Jo asked his new flame.

She tried to figure it out.

— Let's start with the ones we're sure of. Number 1, let's say, that's a wealthy one, unknown, the "Boss" they are talking about, at the top of the chain. Number 2, Prince Marty. Number 3, Gerry the redhead. Number 4, Anatoly the Chechen. Number 5, 6… key intermediaries in Istanbul, Socotra?

— Ok, but there need to be more. Number 7 and 8, at least one main crook in charge in Mozambique and one in Zanzibar. And let's talk about two other key guys, on the boats? Say we're at 10. My grandfather was working as a longshoreman at the Istanbul docks in Turkey and had seen cargos of all types; he would say, I think, that with 10 ferocious bandits, enough money, and 2 or 3 more key people somewhere at the beginning of the chain and at the end of the chain, you were all set for an interesting smuggling piece of work, with relatively low risk.
— Do we also need to find now the final buyers on site. I mean they're actors for the Princes Marties. You know what I mean?
— Yes, but not easy to find, and do we have enough meat to send to Barker?
— Think so. And do we also ship this info to Interpol, to the CIA... or let Barker do it himself?
— I don't know. In fact, we might want to write to all of them, including those to Interpol, and tell them to contact Barker too, since he already believes us.
— What day are we?
— Friday, June 18. The operation in Smolensk is up for when, today...? Or was it all for yesterday? Well, I blame love for mixing me all up!

Mandy hugged him. Then, he spoke.

— And in Smolensk, they're 8 hours ahead of us here.
— Okay. We need to act now.

— It's already too late to stop them in Smolensk. But they may not have the collaboration of the Russian police though. Remember the Litvinenko intrigue in London in 2008, the poisoning by Polonium 210?
— Yes, I do. Indeed, the Russians did not collaborate at all with the UK in the case. Put sand in the gears.
— Let's write the letter anyway and write down a complete description of our knowledge of the affair, from A to Z, but not how we learned of it, of course. Just write that we know it, that's it, that's all, and learned about this from a contact at a very high level, say at the UN. Does that sound logical?
— Yep, works for me, Jo said. We may even not mention any source.

They tried to stay as anonymous as possible. They created a whole new Hotmail address, with fake references, and sent it to the Interpol in London, to Jeune Afrique and to Le Monde, to the Independent and to The Guardian, to the International Herald Tribune, the Los Angeles Times, and a few others.

And, the brown envelope text was delivered to Barker.

The other messages sent by e-mail, with all the details they had.

Time was a key factor.

Even if Barker knew, and had known for some time, that the operation was about to start, or was already going on.

Killings in Smolensk

Friday, June 18, 6:15 in the morning in Smolensk, Russia.

Dimitri Salenko was about to sip his coffee, then leave to the Smolensk warehouse.

He had been working there since 1975 and was now 75 years old. Tons of water had flowed under the bridges.

He'd seen the USSR collapse, but, of course, not the Bolshevik revolution in 1917. He was born in 1935. His first clear memories were about the war. 1943: the Stalingrad battle. They'd resisted Hitler. His father did not like Joseph Stalin, as so many Russians did, but never spoke about it.

Dimitri's wife woke up and went into the kitchen to kiss him.

He thought he knew what was in this warehouse, one of the few not dismantled since the 1989 Berlin wall fall, then the collapse of the USSR. In his mind, it was radioactive stuff, inspected once in a while by engineers.

With five other guys, they rotated surveillance of the warehouse and surroundings to assure security. Seven days a week. Few holidays. A holy job, in this fragile world.

Very exceptionally, a seventh man was used. At all times, two guys were on site.

He hadn't really understood why somebody would try to steal, damage or even play with radioactive waste. Of course, he was not aware that arms were inside, not radioactive stuff people thought it was.

But he was honestly paid, and the warden job was easy enough to often play cards during hours with the other guard, so why complain?

- You're now close to retirement, his wife said, getting herself a cup of coffee and sitting down alongside her husband. You told me, last year... Okay, I'm reaching retirement, getting older; we no longer need so much money since we don't travel anymore. Our children have been on their own for many years, and my pay had been stable. This is what you told me, remember?
- Yes, honey, you're still teaching, and younger than I am. Yes, of course I should be off next year. Doesn't mean I want to retire so much. I love my job.
- And, by the way, when will the Russian government take care of this waste, and how?
- Don't know, Svetlana. Don't know. Okay, we have to decide on a date. Say on December 24th. Okay?
- Okay. Have a nice day. Kisses. And beat young Viktor at blackjack! As you pretend you usually do.

Viktor Gromirovski had also worked there since a long time. Although much younger than Dimitri, they were good friends.

He was born in 1960 and was hired at the warehouse when he was eighteen, in 1978. He'd worked there all his life and was now fifty.

His wife Tatiana and his two daughters, Sammy and Marta, said goodbye to their father.

— Have a nice Saturday! Try to beat the old Dimitri.
— Thanks girls. Have fun out on the soccer field today.
— What time are you back?
— Close to 6, as usual.

***

The Outskirts of Smolensk, Russia. June 18th, 6:30 a.m. The door of a small motel room opened.

Anatoly the Chechen went out to the foggy coffee shop. He had to meet with a few ferocious guys.

Then pick two, young, nervous boys, the best Clark's lift drivers in Smolensk, and probably in the whole Western Russia. They were Ukrainians, though he was not sure.

The boys were going to be there for a long trip because they were the kings of forklifts operators, and would be so well paid.

In fact, they received their allowance in advance, in US dollars, for a normal three days of eight hours of work. But they would also receive double their usual hourly rate, for the additional number of hours needed.

They were told they would have to be very swift because a foreign boat was about to be in the harbor for a short while, and refrigerated goods had to be transported quickly from the warehouse to trucks, then from trucks onto these vessels.

Nothing so unusual for the boys, except for the pay. They hadn't questioned much; money talks, and they'd accepted the job.

At 9:40, Dimitri and Viktor were playing cards.

Every twenty minutes or so, they'd take a walk around the warehouse, as they had done for so many years. Nothing to declare, as usual.

Back from one of those walks, they played a last blackjack round before their sandwich break, which was usually left in their pickup truck, an old black Ford F-150 Dimitri had owned since the 1980s. Few Fords in Russia, but some of these old nuggets here and there.

At 9:55, exactly, Dimitri went out to the Ford.

Viktor waited at the small table where they played cards.

Dmitri walked slowly, with deliberation. He knew somebody could try to steal something, be it the table itself, the little heating equipment he had, partly outside the building, or anything else they could get their hands on. Though, highly unlikely.

Once, recently, two young boys came around, unarmed, claiming the cash they thought that was inside the warehouse. Dimitri showed them his gun, and they ran away, terrified. Around ten minor incidents in more than thirty years, but nothing close to be an emergency.

He reached the pickup at 9:58.

Viktor could no longer see him, as he'd turned the corner of the building.

The Chechen stepped out from the woods, twenty feet in front of him, pointing a Kalashnikov.

Not a good idea for Dimitri to take out his gun.

He had an emergency number, sure, but there was no chance now.

— This is what you think it is, an attack. Be cool and nothing will happen to you. Anatoly said, softly. How many guards are with you?

Dimitri immediately knew it was serious.

He thought about his wife and daughters who would be left.

He thought about the good life he'd had, despite, of course, Stalin, Khrushchev, Brezhnev, Gorbachev, Yeltsin and a few other leaders he had hated so much.

— One.
— Where's the other guy? He has guns?
— Yes, Viktor wears it. He's right around the corner, sitting at a table. What do you want?
— Don't fool us. If you pull anything, we will kill you instantly, or worse, torture you a bit before. We want the keys of the warehouse, to take contents we need before 5 o'clock, and then leave. Now, let's go get your friend.

Dimitri hesitated a second. He could yell as hard as he could, warning Viktor to run for his life.

But he would be killed; having alerted Viktor, but is that dying for nothing? Helping his friend? Maybe he would save Viktor, but not sure at all.

Moreover, the Chechen was certainly not alone: his crooks' band probably all around, so Viktor would have no chance to escape.

He did not yell.

He tried for another plan to survive, playing the game with the Chechen.

— What about us, afterward?
— We'll see. Now, for the keys.
— I have the first set, Viktor, the second. Once in, a special alarm system will trigger if we get inside the closed and secured area.
— I already know that. You'd have said anything else, and I could have killed you on the spot. We are plugged in higher, so the alarm system will reach nobody.

They went to get Viktor, advancing slowly to the corner.

Dimitri first, hands up over his head, and the Chechen following him, twenty feet behind.

When Viktor saw them, Dimitri spoke first.

— Viktor, don't take your gun. These guys are serious and very dangerous.
— Okay, I see.

At that moment, other lascars came out of the bushes, all around them, five guys, armed to the teeth. Two trucks could be loaded at the same time, the Chechen had managed. That's why they'd brought along the two quick lift guys.

The alarm system, in fact, was not one that worked with noise. It only sent a message, somewhere, somehow. And, today, somebody would ignore it, and take it as the signal that the Dark Snakes Operation had started in Smolensk.

The warehouse was opened thanks to Dimitri and Viktor. They then unlocked other inside doors, leading to boxes and small containers. The first two truck vans, forty-five feet long, then backed up in front of the doors and opened their own.

The two lifts started to work. The young boys were really quick. Boxes were unloaded, but the contents weren't revealed, since smaller, 4×8 boxes, very heavy, contained the goods to be loaded.

Around 11:40, the first two trucks were full. They had done the same go-in, go-out job, and the engines were going non-stop, taking boxes, rising up on the lift tracks, carefully but quickly transferred into the trucks. There was precision in their work. The Chechen and the other crooks apparently knew exactly what they had to do, what quantity of boxes they would carry on the truck, how exactly to place the stuff into the truck, and so on.

The team other guys, except the drivers, were probably only hit men or professional killers.

At 2 p.m., four trucks were almost fully loaded. One was left. Only one lift was able to work at one time, this warehouse section and the last truck too narrow for two.

At this time, the youngest lift guy, Yuri, a little slower than the other one at operating, understood what was maybe coming for him.

Just before entering the truck with one of the last boxes, he jumped from the open side of the lift, and disappeared into the woods.

One thug left his check on his driver and ran after him. The Chechen ordered loudly.

— Try to keep him alive! May still need him!

The young lift guy was running swiftly, dodging trees and rocks. He escaped fast, went over a boulder but hadn't evidently seen the cliff coming.

He jumped in, probably to his death, maybe seventy feet down, along the mountain crags, through some bushes, to where a small river, a tributary of the Dnieper, reached those bushes.

— We lost him. He's dead, on the banks of the river, way below, explained the crook to the Chechen.
— Bad news. We may need another liftman in Kherson, for putting the boxes onto the boats.

Dimitri took out his phone and, as the guards weren't looking, sent a short text message: *"We were highjacked."*

The Chechen saw him, thirty feet away. He fired three times.

Dimitri fell down. He was mortally hurt.

He just had time to close the phone, erase the last text message before Anatoly came over. When he did, on the ground, Dimitri was laying, smiling, dying.

— Thanks, sir, good luck with this radioactive garbage, he said.

The Chechen fired two more bullets. But not in the face, only to avoid having him suffer too long. Anatoly was not so bad?

Fierce, but because of the circumstances in Chechnya, he used to say, that's the reason: to protect his mom and family.

He took Dimitri's phone but couldn't see his last text message sent. He was furious.

— Let's load the rest! Hurry!

At 4:45 pm, the last truck was done.

They had put several boxes of dishes and tableware in the rear of the cargo. In case of an inspection on the road, they would open a few boxes to the police. If needed, they would shoot, of course.

Strangely, there were old dishes in the warehouse, waiting. The Chechen identified the boxes, apparently, as they were a slightly different color. As it turned out, someone had prepared many months, or even years, for this "sale"?

When they finished loading the shipment, they asked Viktor, shaking, to close the warehouse. As if nothing had occurred. One crook had taken care of Dimitri's body and was removing the blood, carefully washing the place.

— Now, what about me? Said Viktor. You're going to kill me now or later?

— You drive these Clark's lifts? How well?
— Yes, said Viktor. Quite well. I had a second job, and still do it part time.
— Okay, I want to see this now.

Viktor was right. He showed them how. Indeed, he was very good, made no errors, for few minutes of testing.

— And I am a mechanic, too. Not only know how to operate these lifts but how to fix them right, just in case. I'll bring my tools from my car if you want. And some all-fit parts.

The Chechen took one second, then spoke.

— Okay, take your tools. And let's go. Go into truck number two.

Viktor did as he was told. He made sure to push with his left foot, just in front of the doors, a few small red rocks, an unusual element. Hopefully, the guards coming at 5:30 could see these. It could help the local police to search for them a little more quickly, since they would not meet with Dimitri and Viktor for the work wardens change, as they usually did, too. Could.

They left.

With five trucks, tons of light arms, grenades, everything.

And with one body to throw into the Dnieper or the dump, a few miles away.

***

New York, Saturday, June 19th, 7 a.m.

Jonathan woke up. He'd have to go to work at 6 pm, but Mandy was off.

He kissed her softly and returned to sleep for a while. At 7:45, he was preparing coffee.

— Hello. Had a good night, princess?
— Yes, sure! Black please. Where do you want me to put your tip?
— Here, he said, showing his left cheek.

They had breakfast and later started a long walk, hand in hand, in the rain. They almost said nothing, enjoying the present moment. Just… living, breathing in the Manhattan drizzle.

Back from this long, lovely walk, they immediately went to the newspapers, on the web.

— Which one do we look at? She asked.
— First, the Smolensk Herald, Moscow Times, then, and IHT, NYT, maybe some other news source.
— What do you expect to find?
— Not sure what, news of the killings or kidnapping of the guards, something, nothing, maybe, let's see.

The Smolensk Herald had only two articles written in English, the remaining in Russian.

The two lovers didn't find anything there.

The Kiev Post, a newspaper that had been printed in English too since 1995, had several interesting articles. The first was about Gas-Prone and Naftogas about to merge operations.

Jonathan and Mandy understood: the huge Gas-Prone Russian company was to swallow another energy producer.

Jo and Mandy were aware of Russian politics, the turning on and off of the valve of natural gas by Gas-Prone, a big energy provider to Western Europe, and Ukraine. Knocking to their knees giants like Germany and France in negotiation on natural gas prices and supply, particularly during fall and winter. Nothing new but another big move by Gas-Prone. Related to their story? Maybe.

He turned to Mandy.

— Did you know Gas-Prone was a crown society in the USSR and had been sold for less than 1% of its real value, to several oligarchs, during the Yeltsin years?
— Where did you find all that info?
— An investigative journalist wrote a book about it, and much more. A genius for smelling the bullshit. He found plenty of information, published a lot but was killed in the streets in the early 2000s, in Moscow's city center.
— So, Gas-Prone is still an instrument of power in Russia?
— Not only *an* instrument of power. Maybe *the main* instrument of power.
— Okay, great. Related to our story?

— Don't know. Maybe. Maybe not. Let's keep on doing the research and read a bit more.

They went on searching, head-to-head, hand-in-hand, each using remaining hand to click or point, through the web.

The Kiev Post had a small column on murders and deaths of the day. Along advertising nice Ukrainian women looking to meet older, richer men from America or Western Europe, the murders were written out as a list.

The Post's murder column was interesting. A young Ukrainian man, Danil Lutchenko, was found dead in Smolensk.

He'd fallen from a 75 feet cliff. Without apparent reason.

The journalist had talked to his mother, and she was terribly upset. Danil was a lift operator, a daily worker. The funerals would be held two days later, in Kiev. No journalist had signed the article, the Kiev Post only. There was nothing about it being close or not to a warehouse.

They kept on for news about the strike at the Kherson and Odessa harbors. Strikes were confirmed. They'd be sending info to Barker today.

Real chaos at the harbors, according to the Post, probably for many days to come. Anastasia Poumirova had written the article. A real muckraker when it came to top Russia politics.

They decided to send the name and article to Barker, too.

Poumirova wrote she didn't understand the how and why of this strike. She knew the employees at the docks were among the best paid, unskilled workers in the country, even with good retirement benefits, adequate worker's compensation insurance and other insurance, like dental and medical, in their working conditions. Still rare in Russia. Strange. So, why a strike?

Amanda managed to write the letter to place in the brown envelope, as Jo continued to search.

A Moscow Times article was appropriate, today.

The reporters noted the Smolensk incident, but added that it happened very close to a murky warehouse, of unknown content. But, officially, they said, it was holding some remains of the Chernobyl nuclear catastrophe in 1986.

They included words on the missing of the two guards, one later found floating on the Dnieper. He'd been identified as Dimitri Salenko, his wife testified; she'd talked to the Moscow Times.

But the local police really appeared heading to close the story as soon as possible, as they often did. They said an autopsy wouldn't be requested by the family, denied by Salenko's wife. The Moscow Times journalist said he'd been thrown off the case.

No words about the incident from international newspapers, nor the NY Times, nor from Reuters, nor from the France Presse, nor from any other newspaper agency. Yep, it was a local incident, indeed.

So, even more important to include details about it for Barker and others.

At 5 p.m., Mandy had finished writing.

— I'll leave it at the NY Times, she said.

I'm back onto Jeune Afrique. They have an article about Mozambique! He said.

— What?
— Yes. Here it is: "Security forces dispersed a crowd that had gathered in Pemba, fired tear gas, chasing the protesters away… a group of people said they'd formed an advisory committee to modify the laws in the country and get a vote on a new draft constitution. The actual president supports it, wants to scrap the actual constitution, write a new one. Things appear in a chaos."
— Interesting enough. Should we include it in the brown envelope?
— Sure. Should we ask Barker to insert words, say "Constitution" and "Potatoes" in his next paper, to say he got all the info? And start with, "Today, I…" to signal us things are going well in their investigation, and with "Next year," somewhere, if things aren't going so well?
— Okay. Good idea.

At 5:30, Mandy left, and Jo went to the DD. At 6:30, surprise.

Barker entered the DD, along with another man.

Jo went over, offering the upper table. They said, yes, why not this nice spot. Minutes later, three pretty young women came inside. Jo managed to give them the table at the lower level.

The perfect setup, once more.

— Hey, where are you from? Your favorite drink? I can bring it right over.
— Sure. Arkansas. Two miles away from Bill Clinton's childhood home. We'll take two Baileys, please.
— Great.

Listening to the men. Barker talking first.

— Don't know where all this info's coming from: no hints, no fingerprints, a careful job, these brown envelopes. And all the included info seems fine, maybe not perfect, but detailed, a leak from inside, maybe?
— Yep, possible, let's see all the developments.
— I'll call the office right now; they may have received other secrets.

At the lower table:

— Bill Clinton's house, when he was a young boy, a big mansion?
— No! Quite modest!

From the upper table:

— Another brown envelope? Barker was talking with someone at the NYT Office.
— Yes. Killings and suspect operation near the place the warehouse is located in Smolensk. Good proofs. Interpol could love it. But time plays against us.

Jo went back to the bar, satisfied. He noted the other guy with Barker. A top man from the Editorial Board at the Times. Very good news. They had only one beer and left. Absolutely no hint as whether they knew anything from the DD source. But why were they here at the DD? Coincidence?

The night at the bar went smooth, then.

Cheerleaders from Wyoming, a Viagra salesman from North Carolina, Asian diplomats, Hollywood and Paris stars, ordinary men from the working class in Connecticut, bureaucrats from Colorado, the Toronto mayor, Kansas Cattle Association representatives, the New Mexico skiing team from Albuquerque, South Dakota hunters, NY City policemen, off-duty, with their wives, Mexico's border agents from the Chihuahua state, a Texas shale-gas businessman, an Idaho major hotel chain owner, two teachers from Portugal, nice crowd, as usual.

The "where are you from" question by Jonathan was almost always answered, triggering a short conversation. And no Chechen. And no Gerry. He closed at 3 a.m. Big tips, six business cards and a few phone numbers from the cheerleaders and from other nice women, two from bureaucrats. What a job he had.

Put things in Billy's updated list? No, no need, at least not yet.

***

Sunday morning, June 20th 6 a.m.
Mandy came into Jonathan's room.

She had earned a key, of course, ever since the bike ride in the Catskills.

Around 7:45, the hazelnut coffee was ready.

— From which country?
— Nothing written about it. Only coffee roasted in Chicago and sent to NY.
— Maybe from Mozambique, or Zanzibar or Tanzania, prepared or supervised by armed children soldiers?
— Maybe. Let's take a look at the news again.

They first took a glance at the schedule they had prepared for running the arms. The operation in Smolensk went a little wrong, because the articles lovers found had suggested crooks probably had to kill or run for the young lift driver. He wouldn't have fallen off the cliff without reason. Chased there, Mandy thought, or pushed.

They read the newspapers attentively. Found a bit more.

A short dozen lines from the Independent, in London. They mentioned the incident in Smolensk. The headline was, "Another Easy Closed Case in Russia, this time in Smolensk." They said the police should, maybe, investigate a little more about the case of a young lift driver, apparently falling down a cliff, alone, without reason. And they mentioned the Russian police refused to collaborate with the Interpol, in another unrelated case.

— Good news, I think, said Jonathan.
— Don't see how, explain, Sherlock Holmes.

— Well, look. The Independent, the newspaper, may have received our info. They may not want nor can provoke the Russian police on that case. But they may want to kind of talk to us, saying that some Interpol is involved, somehow. That's what I read.
— Interesting. Possible. Let's see Barker's column.
— Barker! I almost forgot about him. So stupid.

Barker started with keywords, "Today, on June 20th, I'm celebrating the birthday of one of my dear nephews."

— Nice! So, their investigation is working. He embraced her. Hoping for the best.

Even if they suspected the worse for the Smolensk warehouse guards, and knew it for a young, honest, lift driver, and for innocent populations somewhere in Africa.

— You remember the movie, *Warlord*, about Viktor Bout, an international arms dealer?
— Yes, it starts by saying, more or less, "On this earth, one person out of twelve owns a firearm. The arms makers are asking themselves what to do in order to arm the eleven others."
— Yep. And we're not talking here about honest hunters.
— Indeed.

They discussed all they thought what was about to happen, or intended, as far as the crooks' plans go.

The plans: to travel through the Ukraine border, then to Kherson or another port on the Black Sea, all by road. Next, the trans-shipment from trucks to boats. How many boats? One, two? More? Or, perhaps, only one to Socotra Island, then to be split in two, or three, to Zanzibar and Mozambique, or there would be more smaller boats.

Who knows?

The news were not helpful here.

Tired of searching, Jonathan shared with Mandy the "beef" cards game rules and simulated a game.

As if they were four of them sitting around a table, playing.

Someday, he said, you'll come with me for a visit to Vermont; you'll play this wonderful beef cards game with Mom and Dad, or someone else, the neighbors maybe, at home.

Then, when and if you do, you'll definitely impress them, he added, smiling.

They went to visit Bryant Park, walked around. Jo was in the bar at six. Busy.

But almost zero conversation went on this night for him, except a Russian dignitary coming to the usual table. He talked, talked, and talked. Jonathan heard nothing related to the Smolensk case, nor to the project.

Possibly an honest diplomat. Jo was happy to see there were probably still a lot like him.

Tens, hundreds, thousands, he hoped. He closed at 2 in the morning.

$800 in tips.

He'd been depositing money into several different banks, savings accounts. Give a part to NGO's.

And had considered sharing the bike collection work with Mandy.

Or start an antique store, in his future home in Vermont, with a clay tennis court on site, full of happy friends, young people, playing there.

And Mandy as a double's partner, or an opponent in singles? He smiled to himself.

***

Monday, June 21st.

A stop to throw Dimitri's body into the Dnieper.

Because the dump was not accessible, too muddy. Cement blocks attached to his feet, roped to them.

Then the trucks headed south, toward the Ukrainian border.

Somehow, they'd done it wrong. The body promptly resurfaced and floated onto the shore of a private cottage summer property, whose owners called the police immediately.

The crooks had two choices: the largest border post or a much smaller one.

If the larger one, maybe there would be very few questions, as the traffic was heavy, and the Ukrainian employees inspected about one truck out of every thirty. Even in this case, they could only open the first few boxes, look into it, and let them go. But if trouble came, the police would be quickly on site, and it was probably impossible to bribe all the agents; there would be too many. If the smaller post, then it would be the reverse: the higher probability of inspection but much easier to bribe. The mileage was about the same.

They opted for the smaller post.

So, the Chechen's truck was the last of the five in the chain.

He was calmly giving orders the other teams, by cellphone.

In each truck was: the driver, one crook with a loaded gun, often pointing on the driver, and a few other hit men inside the cabs.

In number five, the remaining Clark's lift guy, Guennady Oulianov, was sitting right to the driver and the gunman, in the backseat, with Anatoly.

He knew he could be killed if he tried to escape.

But he also knew that the Chechen would prefer not to murder him, since he was the best guy on the lifts, had clocked in 5,000 miles all around. And job remained to be done.

The drivers all had international driver's licenses and were excellent.

This was no time to get into an accident. If that happened, however, the Chechen would have to decide what to do, and would only have seconds to do so. This was one of the most perilous parts of the journey.

And rollover of a truck would be a catastrophe. If one was about to get into a serious accident, bribing was the first option, so that the police wouldn't open the cargo, and even collaborate to have the whole group of trucks back to the road quickly.

Shooting off guns was the last option, but they may have no choice.

The farther the border was, the less shooting and killings was an option.

They had chosen to cross the Ukrainian border between Belgorod, in Russia, and Alysivika, in Ukraine, two quiet small cities north of Kharkov. There was that much more populated city in Ukraine, Kharkov, to go through, after.

Then they had to head south to Dnipropetrovsk, then to Kherson, both in Ukraine.

They would have to rest somewhere, probably around Alysivika, close to the border Russia-Ukraine, or south of Kharkov, two or three hours after the border checks.

The drivers and the crooks had along pills to avoid sleeping, but they had their limits.

The guys would rent only two motel rooms, with a communicating door. The Chechen would alternate the night guard with one another armed guy, at the motel.

All trucks stopping at the motel, altogether.

They would pause only 3 hours for a short sleep. The drivers were quite used to this schedule, always drinking from their big mugs of very strong coffee. There'd be probably no sleep at all for Anatoly.

The journey went smoothly until the border.

***

The small Ukrainian border gate, near Belgorod, was rarely used by many trucks from the same company, certainly not five.

This journey from Smolensk was longer by Belgorod than by, say, by Kiev or by Kremenchuk. Much longer.

In fact, the Chechen had stopped twice, both times in Sudzkato, to get a lot of cocaine bags worth a few million bucks, for his own personal profit. He would leave them in Merefa, just south of Kharkov, the center of the illegal Chechen activities in Ukraine, a small city unknown to almost everybody except to all Chechens.

At Belgorod border crossing, Anatoly had to declare their contents, where they were going, including the final destination.

All trucks stopped along the road, one kilometer before the border.

There, the Chechen truck went first. Anatoly, 6 foot 2, 200 pounds, impressive, in the passenger seat, and all dressed as a delivery truck driver, declared some office furniture, some chairs and tables. He told them, coming from Smolensk, going to Kherson.

The two local agents, only two, asked some questions. But then, things went weird.

The agents felt there was something wrong with the declaration. 5 trucks was odd.

At random, they chose the fifth truck to open and inspect.

Trouble was, that was exactly, in the fifth truck, where the Chechen had loaded the cocaine.

At this point, Anatoly went outside.

He took one of the guards aside, talking friendly, and turned the corner of the building, so he was no longer visible.

Everybody knew something was going on, but, what, they didn't know. They all waited.

The Chechen put his gun against the border guard's head.

— You have a choice. $30,000$ US, and let us go, or a series of bullets in your nice, little pretty Ukrainian head, right now. Think quick. I prefer to give you the money. What about you? Money or bullets?
— Money please.

The Chechen pulled off his gun, took thirty bills, $1000 each, counted, gave only fifteen to her.

— So, now you're going to go back and let us pass. Simple enough?
— Sure. But what... what about the remaining $15,000? She asked, shaking.
— We know your address. You have two children, Mikaëla and Andreï. You will receive it, once in a while, in exchange for your silence. Share a bit with the other guard. Understood?
— Yes.

Five minutes later, they were inside Ukraine.

And both guards a bit richer. Many years of salary. She would not talk. Feeling a gun against your head makes you think.

Anatoly the Chechen now had to manage the cocaine.

When they passed Kharkov, he asked for the trucks to stop near Merefa.

They did so outside a little sordid motel, with the crooks watching the drivers, along with Guennady, who was still thinking about the least risky way to escape. But he could see no opportunity.

The Chechen exchanged ten big cocaine bags for two million US dollars, and few words, with another Chechen, with same composure, same eyes.

— Hi, old bro.
— Hi, young bro.
— Do you have the "material"?
— Yes, Anatoly said. But wait. Before the cam, tell me. How is Mom in Grozny?
— Fine.
— You have a recent photo? From this week, dressed as I requested?
— Yes. Here it is.
— Fine, bro, Anatoly said to his brother, carefully looking at his mother's photo. Take the bags. Do what you have to do.
— Anatoly, you know me. I will never screw you over.
— I know, and you have to protect Mom from these ugly Russians bastards. Never forget. And I would not forgive you.
— Yes, I know; you've told it one hundred times, Jordi said, laughing a little.

For the first time in months, a short smile adorned Anatoly the Chechen's face.

— Jordi, you know I do not trust anybody. Except, you, my own young brother. But you too, never trust anybody; promise me again?
— Including you?
— Not including me.
— Promised. No one except you.

They exchanged the cash and the cam.
Then hugged, and each went his separate way, Anatoly to the motel, and Jordi to who knows where.

***

Inside the motel, everything was fine.
Now, we have to sleep. Nobody objected.

***

Three hours later, the crew started toward Kherson. The road was quiet, but a few incidents along the way. Maybe once or twice, a car cut into their lane, the driver possibly drunk, but the Chechen's truck drivers were used to it, and avoided the imminent crash, honking, their foot down on the brakes on time.

About forty miles before a key road intersection, Anatoly received a call.

— Hell keeper speaking.
— This is Gerry. You have to change the plans. Listen to me, Anatoly.
— Okay. Go ahead, Gerry.

— You're going to Odessa, instead of Kherson, Gerry the redhead said. Higher orders.

Fierce Crooks

Sevastopol, on the Crimean peninsula, was the original real destination.

Only the Chechen and Gerry knew, in order to be sure nobody would talk.

It was a far longer journey by road from Smolensk, but shorter to Istanbul by sea.

Then it had changed to Kherson, and now to Odessa.

— Damn it, Gerry. Why this change in plans again?
— Higher orders. Much higher. From London, you know.
— The great, great boss?
— Yes. You have to sell some arms I will tell you and munitions in Odessa, to guys from Tiraspol, Transnistria. They will meet you.
— Gerry, you know how much more dangerous this is? And we have to be a lot more prudent in Odessa than in Sevastopol or even Kherson, and then probably sail along the Romanian and Bulgarian coast. This no longer the Nicolae Ceausescu era as you well know! These countries, particularly Romania, now, are running more and more

stringent checks on boats! Tell the great boss to go to hell with this plan change; I'm not at all certain about this choice, and why.
— Wait, Anatoly. I cannot tell the great boss to go to hell. Nor you can. You probably need at least $1 million more in bribes of all kinds, just to get through Istanbul, then through the Suez Canal, Socotra and then to the final destinations. You may even need more, you know, to deal with the Somalian pirates.
— Very dangerous, I repeat... very dangerous, these guys from Tiraspol are even worse than Russians, if it exists.
— He's ordered it, Gerry. And if we don't comply, he will launch a "Wanted, Dead or Alive" against you, starting in the next few minutes. Even your own guys can betray you.
— Humm. Okay, let's go to Odessa, then.

The trucks were fully packed. But an idea went through his head. Sell or give a part of the arms to his brother, for Chechnya's struggle against Russia.

Not to the Tiraspol guys. Nobody would know.

— Ok, not so hard. The warehouse didn't fill the five trucks entirely, so it should be easy to unload some to these rotten Transnistrian guys. I know exactly where is every little thing in the contents, Anatoly said to Gerry.

— Okay then, said Gerry. Go to dock 201, at 10 a.m. tomorrow. You still have the Clark's lift ready, in the back of one truck?
— Sure. Who's paying?
— They will pay on site, cash. In US dollars. Be prudent, of course, but get it.
— Humm, even more risky. But Okay. Then, on to Odessa, dock 201.

Immediately after, he called Jordi.

— Brother, Anatoly here again.
— Mom is still fine, I swear...
— Okay, great. Find a 30 feet truck, empty. And go to Otchakiv port along the Black Sea. Be there in two hours. I'll call you about the exact place on the harbor, but it's small.
— Yes. I'm familiar with this harbor. So, tell me: for what, why?
— A gift for your little disputes against the Moscow dirty dogs. Worth $200 million, say. From me. Or from Santa Claus if you want. Is Stanislas still in Otchakiv? We're on the road with this gift.
— Stan died last year. Gun shots to the chest. And I cannot make it. I go to Kiev. But his son Valery will do.
— As ferocious as Stan?
— Much more. And loyal.
— Deal for using Valery. You'll have to bring it back to Grozny. Then probably a part to Uzbekistan, later; I'll tell you when.

— Count on me and Valery.

They started toward Odessa, making a quick stop in Otchakiv, to unload half-truck for Valery.

Anatoly and Valery met, face to face. Valery was a small man, muscled, with icy eyes, an iron-man.

— Valery.
— Anatoly. Hi. Friends of my friends are friends.
— I no longer have friends, Anatoly said. This dirty civil war against Russia's mob changed all that. I have contacts. Only a few positive ones. You are now one.
— Anabella wants to say hello.
— Tell her I miss her. And love her. In the way I can. I should be back some weeks from now, or this fall. Say hi to my son. How old is he now?

Even a guy like Valery could hardly believe it. Chechnya's strange war against Russia had transformed Anatoly into a wild animal, not knowing how old his own son was.

— Seven. How much does Chechnya owe you for this gift?
— It's free. I have no friends, no longer a heart I believe, but a loyalty to those who have suffered and are still suffering in that dirty war against Russia. I only really love Mom, Anabella, and my son. Several of Mom's friends have died making explosives that they blew up in a suicide kamikaze,

somewhere in Russia, for the cause. They should not have done things this way. But all of Chechnya needs hundreds of million dollars to survive, and from where I'm staring at the thing, I see no other way to make a difference than with what I'm doing now.

— Granted, Anatoly. They hugged and left.

The convey rode easily until Odessa, without any problems. Nobody said anything.

But Anatoly sang a few Chechen songs of his youth, and some of the Beatles: *Let It Be*, *Yesterday*, sometimes for everybody, in his cell phone, here and there.

A few guys sang, too, when they knew parts.

***

Odessa, Wednesday morning, June 23rd, dawn. Chilly winds, not usual, for the season.

Tiraspol merchants were not those expected, not those whom Anatoly knew.

They paid half right away. But they asked to load the truck themselves, with their own lift. Their own guy.

Having suspected the worse, Anatoly had placed a few snipers just over the place, hired two hours before by Valery. His trigger words for the snipers were: "*NOT SURE.*"

A group of five mercenaries stood in front of Anatoly's team. All wearing guns, in hand. With their boss.

— Let's do it with our own machine, our way, the Tiraspol guys leader said.

Anatoly was annoyed.

— Why? We have the fastest, safest lift guy in whole Russia, the Chechen said.
— Maybe, but we do not trust him. Would you accept the following: first half, our guy on it; second half, your guy?
— Well, "*NOT SURE*," Anatoly said, loudly.

Seconds later, all the Tiraspol men were dead, shot by the elite snipers on the top of the adjacent building.

They found the second half of the money in a big bag, close behind the dead guys, under a tree.

— Let's go, NOW! Anatoly yelled.

And, so, a few minutes later, having stuffed the bodies into nearby garbage bins, they ran off for the harbor, 20 minutes away.

The boats were ready, and Gerry the redhead, the little Vermonter from Richford, was there, at the dock, waiting for the Chechen's group.

— Hi, Anatoly. Problems somewhere?

Anatoly was prepared. This time he'd use the partial truth.

Gerry was a kind of right arm of the London boss. Prudence.

— Yes. Killed six guys, 10 minutes ago. But no trouble. No noise. These new, long guns from Afghanistan have one of these silencers...
— Okay. I partly expected this. Somehow, they knew you had an important load, and they wanted to take it all, maybe. So, nice job. How much are three snipers worth, for six dead guys, here?
— Half the Moscow price. $10,000 US each. The Tiraspol guys paid, though, before unloading, so we have all the money, they were stupid, but had it on them, maybe for another operation soon.
— Oh, Gerry said. Sure, I guess they expected to get it back from you, killing you, nice piece of work, Anatoly.

Two hours later, the boat was ready.

It was much easier to move stuff from trucks into an open boat than from a tiny warehouse with narrow corridors into the vans.

Viktor, not bad at driving lifts, helped in the loading. Just before he finished, Anatoly had to decide.

Give Viktor a bullet to the back of the head. Or let him go free.

— Viktor. I have a choice, now, to make, concerning you.

— I know. Do it now. Don't make me suffer: this is all I ask. I had a good life. Thanks be to God if I am leaving now.
— I know too. You have a wife, children in Smolensk. Keep silent. We will protect you. As much as we can. Try to contact your family now, then start a new life outside Smolensk.
— Thanks, Anatoly.
— But forget all of this and my name. Take this $20,000 USD for your trip back and some chocolates and flowers, and this fine little coffee bag from Brazil, and a few other things, to give to your wife. Sorry about Dimitri. It's all business, you know. The civil war with Russia.
— Okay, sir. Sad, but I understand for Dimitri. Thanks for everything. God bless you.
— You'll have to keep hidden, traveling for six days or so. Back in Smolensk, try to vanish somewhere, but if you can't, tell the police, if you're asked, that you were kidnapped and brought here. They will probably know all this anyway. You didn't hear any names, keep your talk to a minimum, but try to show you are collaborating. Still, they may kill or torture you. Or both. I'm planning on contacting you later, to know more. I may want you to help us in the future. You will be at risk every day, but alive. Or you die now. You choose. Go, or die. Money or bullets. What's your answer?
— I am going.
— Good luck, Viktor. You're a good man. But remember: soft guys seldom win.

Viktor left.

Who thought? This brutal Anatoly was a good guy, somewhere, deep inside?

The boat started toward Istanbul, on the churning waves of the Black Sea.

***

Monday, June 21

Jonathan was off, and on Tuesday, the 22nd as well.

Amanda was very busy at work and had virtually no minutes for him, nor for bandits.

It was time for Jo to rush onto the net to try to help the Interpol team, Barker, and the African children who would be killed and displaced in Mozambique, and in other African countries most probably. If possible.

Normally, the trucks should have been in Kherson by this time, according to what Jonathan knew.

Then, in Istanbul, getting there by sea. But there was no way he could know the details and the plan changes, of course.

Jonathan started to search the net.

***

Istanbul, Turkey

Tuesday June 23rd, in the a.m.

The boat was the Isaacson and sported along its stern a Liberian insignia. As with many of these ghost ships, with murky contents, did.

The crew was composed of only seven guys aside of the crooks, all from Turkey.

The captain was an older man, who knew everything about seas. Anatoly had used him in the past. If he would have had any friends left, this guy would be one of them, one of the very best friends.

They made the easy trip along the Black Sea, undisturbed. No gale-force winds, no strong waves, nothing serious.

They then entered the Bosporus Strait into which Istanbul jutted. A small inspection ship from the Turkish authorities went to greet them, but the inspectors did not board the Isaacson, only stood on their little boat, having a three-minute discussion about their contents and destination.

Gerry spoke to them in English, and the captain, in Turkish, saying they had used cars and trucks aboard, which was partly true. And they would have to stop in Port Said, at the entrance to the Suez Canal, to deliver them to a local car dealer.

From the Turkish inspection boat, they could see several pick-up trucks and a few other Toyota and Volkswagen vehicles.

A cargo of used cars was not an interesting topic for the Turkish guards. They let them go.

Amanda would have said: a gruyere cheese.

Gerry then went to the coast, in a small, motorized boat. He could take the plane to Cairo, then to Port Said.

He always had things to arrange, bribes to pay, diplomats to corrupt, inspectors to bring to the theater and to the bars, to get them half drunk and close their eyes to unlawful operations.

This time when the Isaacson would go through the Suez Canal, and more, huge amounts of bribes were needed. At this, Gerry was a master, and earned hundreds of thousands of dollars a year doing it.

The great boss, on high, knew the value of such a lieutenant.

They'd only met twice in person a few years back. But Gerry returned to the boat 40 minutes later.

He had decided to stay on board for the whole crusade. He'd had all of his shadow work done, before.

And a few heavily bribed helpers already on key sites.

The Isaacson then went along the little, wonderful Marmara Sea, which separated the Black Sea and the Bosporus from the Aegean Sea, through the second important strait in Turkey, the Dardanelles, southwest of Istanbul.

But the crew did not look at it.

Except Anatoly, thinking his mother would like to see the Marmara Sea, before going to her grave. He asked the captain to stay closer to the shore than they should, for the view.

He took a few photos and would send her, through Jordi's Messenger or What's App, later. He promised himself he'd bring her, next year, exactly here. With his son and Anabella.

Hope keeps you alive.

Everything went smoothly, with this leg of the trip. No inspection along the Marmara Sea, as they were still in Turkey, technically, so, already inspected.

The Isaacson trip on the Aegean Sea was easy, as well.

The crew passed Karpathos Island and headed toward Egypt, to Port Said. This medium size boat reached Port Said and the entrance to the Suez Canal entrance on Thursday, June 24, without incident.

Nothing occurred at the entrance to the Suez Canal, nor along the canal.

Gerry had paid a great deal of fat bribes to a good number of people, for that key Gordian knot, to swiftly cross the most important canal in the world.

They entered the Red Sea on June 25.

Normally, it would take 38 hours to reach the mythic Bab El Mandeb Strait, or the Wailing Gate, due to the strong, prevailing winds.

The small crew was very nervous. They knew they were transporting a kind of highly corrosive content, and they suspected this because of the Chechen presence, the crooks, hand close to their guns at their hips, at all times. Unidentified boxes, so heavy, and these Turkish guys normally did not travel passed Port Said. This time they were heavily paid, so they said yes to the offer.

The Chechen had opened one box and had taken out Kalashnikovs, one for each crook, one for him, one for Gerry. They had enough bullets for an army.

They had to trust each other. But, out here, anybody killing anybody on the boat would be suicide. Each one needed the other. Up until the final delivery.

Or deliveries.

While searching on his side of the world, Jonathan, realized they would have to go through the Bab El Mandeb.

He had heard for the first time about this key strait, in an old 1964 film, starring Richard Widmark, as the Viking's chief, and Sidney Poitier, as an Arabic Prince. Title: *The Long Ships*. Both were looking to find a legendary, huge gold bell, called the *Mother of Voices*. He'd just happened to see the movie at a cinema that showed old reels, watched it with Mandy a few days before.

The Isaacson, with its Viking name, passed through the Bab El Mandeb. At this point, two small planes could be heard overhead.

Used cars were easy to spot from the air. But the key arms boxes were in the hold of the ship, hidden under other used cars and miscellaneous goods. Nothing happened.

They entered the Aden Gulf, closer to Socotra Island. Socotra was a part of Yemen, and Gerry had good contacts there. A formality.

They'd have to put one third of the contents into a second boat, a smaller and faster one, and the last third into another vessel.

So, the three boats would be travelling separately but staying close to one another. Gerry was on one of them, Anatoly on the second, and another loyal Chechen crook, Risto, would take care of the third, the Isaacson, stopping in Zanzibar. Gerry and Anatoly were heading to Pemba, in Mozambique.

***

In Adibu, on Socotra Island, they worked very quickly.

Guennady, the still indispensable lift operator, once again did a perfect job.

The boats were all fit up for their final destination.

Gerry had been in contact with the great boss, on high, in London, and with Prince Marty's men in Zanzibar. And in Mozambique, where the revolution was ready to be triggered.

This is when one of the men committed an error.

Minutes before leaving the port in Adibu, two crewmembers, a sailor from Turkey and a man from Smolensk, decided to wander off, about a quarter of a mile, to a remote place past the docks, to buy some alcohol, cocaine, and some cigars.

The seller was not alone and, on being paid, just whistled. Two dudes came swiftly from behind with knifes and stabbed the buyers.

Murders were done in silence.

The crook, a Russian from the Smolensk region, and the sailor from Turkey, from Antakya, to be exact, fell down, dead, oceans away from home.

Their family would never hear about this unfortunate event, maybe.

The seller pocketed back his money, the drugs, the cigars, and the vodka. Also took all the money the two dead men had on themselves, and one wedding ring.

This all was done, with no one hearing or seeing anything of it: not the crew, not Gerry, not Anatoly. When the time came to untie the ropes of the boat, they had no minutes to search. The missing were two men, two good men short, that is, but that's all.

These crooks often left the team, off with a nice woman, and maybe they left out of fear, or for any number of reasons. Nothing so unusual, but Anatoly didn't like it, suspecting the worst for these guys.

So, on Saturday morning, June 26th, the three boats left Socotra.

They were to reach Zanzibar, on the main island, and Pemba harbor at about the same time. Expected time of arrival, Sunday, June 27th, at night. There were a few big ifs involved.

If the Somalian pirates would not show up, and if no unexpected ocean storm. So, they would stay together until the usual place for the Somalian pirates to attack was passed, the Equator line. Then, they'd separate.

Nothing at all happened on the sea.

On June 27th, one ship docked in Zanzibar, and the two others reached Pemba in Mozambique on the same day.

In Zanzibar, the Interpol agents were on site.

They were waiting with the Tanzanian police, for the boats.

The crew of the Isaacson was done in the Zanzibar harbor; they had no chance to escape. There was an exchange of fire firing with the police, a short, terrible fight.

Risto the Chechen was injured, not seriously, and captured. Only one other member of the crew came out alive, and Guennady, who had managed to hide in the box the Chechen had previously opened.

When the police inspected that box, Guennady yelled, with the few English words he knew.

— Do not shoot! They kidnapped me.
— Who are you?
— I'm a lift driver from Smolensk, a Russian; not a bandit.

The police hoped Guennady would become an important witness in the international inquiry that would follow.

Risto mentioned he intended to cooperate, too.

***

In Mozambique, there were no arrests. The local police refused to collaborate with the Interpol.

In fact, the police forces were already under the control of the armed rebels.

The revolution took place, the rebels armed with the stuff from Gerry's and Anatoly's boats.

Gerry got paid, took an armored car to who knows where in Mozambique.

Anatoly got paid, as well, and too, vanished from the face of the Earth, for as long as needed.

A few days later, the Russian representative made a declaration that went public.

— *Russia will never forget its global responsibilities across the world. We will never permit killings and bloody revolutions, will avoid them if we can. We do not know yet what exactly happened in Mozambique, but there is no proof at all the Blue Helmets would have prevented these events. We think our decision was a rational one, with the information we had at the time of voting at the UN, and hope for the best for the Mozambique people.*

***

Between June 20th and June 27th, Jo and Mandy had gone thoroughly through international newspapers, including many in Turkish, read and then translated by Mandy.

They had found very little potentially useful information.

But one element proved to be interesting: a relatively small local newspaper from Ankara announced the death of the Turkish sailorman in Socotra: the body was to be brought back by the family in Antakya in the next days.

The story briefly described how he was killed, in the harbor, along with a Russian from Smolensk. The local police had identified both very quickly and contacted the families.

A sailor from Turkey and a Russian from Smolensk had been killed at the same place by the same weapons: a clear clue for Barker, which was key in confirming Gerry's plans and the final destination.

A last brown envelope had been prepared, with a few lines of information, asking for the next Barker column to use the words "*Colorful sea*."

Barker's next column spoke about the crowd at the latest Rolling Stones event in Manhattan. The title was, "A *colorful sea* of people went to see old Mick Jagger's show."

***

On July 1st, early in the morning, there were some big news from the IHT, the Independent, Jeune Afrique, the Kiev Post, and the gloss pages of many other newspapers.

One boat, full of arms worth hundreds of millions of dollars, had been taken by the Tanzanian police.

All this with the help of the Interpol agents in Zanzibar. Hundreds of thousands of children soldiers would not be?

In Africa

But the so-called revolution was sparked in Mozambique. A civil war, in fact.

However, this violence had been avoided in southern Kenya and in Burundi, where the arms should have gone from Zanzibar, first, on small boats, then by land, along rural roads.

Mandy was off that day. But Jonathan was heading to work at 6 p.m. that evening. Mandy went over to his apartment.

He opened his door at 8 that morning. They'd already seen the news from the Independent and from the IHT.

— Half victory, she said.
— Yes. But, you know, I'm only a bartender.
— From this angle, not bad. You've saved so many lives.
— We... *we* saved so many lives. And now, where are we heading to?
— I do not know, but I love you.
— Love you too. Want to visit Vermont soon?

A Round of the "Beef Game"?

A few weeks later, Jonathan was at his parents' home in Richford, with Mandy.

At 7 in the evening, Mom answered the door.

— Jo, somebody you may remember is here, to say hello.

Jonathan was wearing a cap, glasses like John Lennon, that he'd needed for a few months now. He had let his beard and hair grow longer than normal.

Gerry the redhead was at the door.

— Hey, Jonathan! Long time no see! I recently learned the rules of that traditional "beef game"! Could we play it soon?

THE END

Printed in the USA
CPSIA information can be obtained
at www.ICGtesting.com
LVHW021343051023
760085LV00064B/1870